THE

OPPOSITE

OF

GEEK

RIA VOROS

THE OPPOSITE OF GEEK

Scholastic Canada Ltd.
Toronto New York London Auckland Sydney
Mexico City New Delhi Hong Kong Buenos Aires

Scholastic Canada Ltd.
604 King Street West, Toronto, Ontario M5V 1E1, Canada

Scholastic Inc.
557 Broadway, New York, NY 10012, USA

Scholastic Australia Pty Limited
PO Box 579, Gosford, NSW 2250, Australia

Scholastic New Zealand Limited
Private Bag 94407, Botany, Manukau 2163, New Zealand

Scholastic Children's Books
Euston House, 24 Eversholt Street, London NW1 1DB, UK

www.scholastic.ca

Library and Archives Canada Cataloguing in Publication
Voros, Ria
The opposite of geek / by Ria Voros.
Issued also in electronic format.
ISBN 978-1-4431-0484-5
I. Title.
PS8643.O76O66 2013   jC813'.6   C2013-901808-5

6 5 4 3 2 1   Printed in Canada 121   13 14 15 16 17

For DH, always.

DFTBA

New Year's Day —
everything is in blossom!
I feel about average.
— Issa

1

JANUARY SUCKS

*In all my sixteen years,
none has been worse than this — even the one
when I had whooping cough.*

Because

not only did I get soaked by a school bus with a Lamborghini alter ego on the way to school, then had to make it through social studies in wet underwear, but now I need a chemistry tutor. A chemistry force-feeder. A raise-my-fricking-grade-or-I'm-gonna-fail messiah. Which spells emotional, social and spiritual doom. Why can't humans hibernate in winter like bears?

Doom

First thing this morning, Mr. Marchand explained what I already knew: I failed the last chemistry test and my grade is teetering on the edge of a precipice. Much improvement needed (understatement, considering the family standard is A average). Next report card will have to be discussed with parents if things don't change. The word "tutor" is thrown around. Doom doom doom.

But Maybe . . .

My best friend, Nemiah Hershey, finds me in the hall and is suitably consoling. She gets As in everything, and I've stopped secretly holding it against her. It's not like she's got a good work ethic or anything. The grades are accidental. She can't help it.

"Why can't you tutor me?" I whine.

This is desperation: we both know Nemiah's allergic to being a teacher. She looks sadly at her beautiful new suede boots. "They would never go for it, you know that."

She's right. The Powers That Be are all-knowing. I'm hooped.

The Tooth Fairy

Ninety minutes later, I fumble to open my locker, thinking things couldn't get any worse. I'm turning the lock when I hear the tinkling voice of someone I ordinarily like.

"Gretchen, do you have a minute?"

The tooth fairy. This is what Nemiah and I call our guidance counsellor, Ms Long, whose teeth are bigger than a horse's — bigger, in fact, than should be crowded into the face of a person so small. She's not that old, maybe thirties, and tinier than most of the grade eights. Her wrists are thinner than the rope we have to climb in gym. I worry about her tripping in the hall and breaking a hip. Nemiah tells me not to worry so much about other people, especially teachers. The tooth fairy perches beside me as I get my books and close my locker. (She is able to perch while she's standing: this is a mystery.) She asks me about my day so far, my best classes, etcetera. She likes that word. She pronounces it ek-SE-tra.

"I don't have to tell you how well you're doing in English," she says. "Writing, reading, eksetra, those were always my strong suit too." She grins with those huge teeth. I know she understands me — we share a love of poetry. She's my source of haiku. But right now there's something else on her clipboard and I'm waiting for it to pounce.

"Speaking of fun, how's chemistry going?" she asks.

"Love it." Eye roll. "Kill me now."

The hall is almost deserted — the bell will go any second. Not soon enough for me.

"I admire your candour," she says, "but your grade is another thing. Mr. Marchand says he's warned you that it's not looking good. We're going to have to talk with your parents about you getting some help."

"Ugh. I hate help. Can't I just struggle along and wait for a miracle?"

3

She gives me a long look, pardon the pun. "Let's not let this spiral out of control, Gretchen. Do you have a plan for pulling up your grade?"

My stomach turns over a bit. "I'm on it. I already have a tutor lined up."

"Really? Whom?" she asks.

My mouth hangs open, waiting for me to fill it with a name.

And finally the blessed bell rings. I bolt for the classroom door, giving the tooth fairy a big, stupid thumbs-up.

So now I have to find myself a tutor.

Our Mission at Carver Green High School

Please don't feel at home; feel like a paranoid loser.
(And there's something on the back of your shirt they
haven't told you about but keep pointing at.)

Don't expect school to be hard work academically unless
you are a science major or heading for Harvard or Oxford.

Expect school to be hard work socially, personally,
spiritually, symbolically, and any other 'ly' there is.

Really.

The Opposite of Chemistry

The written word. Noble, incomparable English: Shakespeare, Wordsworth, Pound, Heaney, Larkin . . .

I am Gretchen Louisa Meyers and I love writing. It's my word sugar. When I was little, I used to tell my sister stories to keep her from whining while we went on long, deadly family walks. Then I started writing them down in secret notebooks I hid under my mattress. Now I write poems all over the place — on candy wrappers, grocery store receipts, hidden corners of my room — whenever they come to me. Which is all the time. Hence: this book. I'm going to document my life over the next few months — who knows, maybe longer. I'm going to, as they say, poem it up.

My Guys

Haiku is an obsession of mine. Those three little lines of poetry, like the perfect snack. Easy to overlook but once you jump in, addicting.

I happened upon a book of haiku on the tooth fairy's shelf and since then I've been getting my daily dose. My haiku gurus are the best: Bashō, Buson and Issa, masters, long dead and weird as hell. They rock. Consider this:

> *That snail —*
> *one long horn, one short,*
> *what's on his mind?*
> — Buson

The Cliques

Why do they tell you high school is about making friends and finding out who you are, when all you really do is try to not be uncool, and fit into one of the acceptable cliques?

The Top Four:

The Legwarmers

The Drama Queens

Sport-and-Entourage

The Crunchy Granolas

None of these cliques are acceptable to us (i.e., none of them accept us), so Nemiah and I chose to be our own clique: the LOLs.

Low-Down on the Top Four

The Legwarmers are dancers, singers and dancer/singer types with lithe bodies and a large gay contingent on the male side — and this only makes them cooler, like boys dating boys = ticket to Broadway. We like them because they tend to be team players — as long as you sign up to do wardrobe or tech support in the school musical.

The Drama Queens might sound like a sect of the above, but don't be fooled — there is very little acting skill among them. They specialize in blond hair from a bottle, flashing bare shoulders or cleavage, and outrageously expensive skin-tight skinny jeans. Favourite pastimes: bitching about how long they stood in line for their latest commercial audition and announcing which celeb they almost made eye contact with at some fancy grocery store.

Sport-and-Entourage (S&E) is pretty simple: S = big guys with small brains and small guys with big egos, and E = all the sporty or slutty girls who hang off them and wear their t-shirts like they're Prada. Cheerleaders are a sub-sect. There are seldom great things to say about this clique, except when they make Provincials or there's a juicy scandal involving nudity and sports equipment.

The Crunchy Granolas are harmless, meatless and often clueless, but because they are always putting up fairly aggressive posters about animal rights and deforestation, they rub some people the wrong way. And the ones with dreads scare the heck out of the Drama Queens.

The LOLs

Nemiah and I have a pact: we must maintain the integrity of our clique, above all else.

Population: 2

Status: alive, but not on the radar

Cool factor: negligible

Overview: we are not really artsy and hardly sporty and a little bit funny, but mostly we are unknown. Those of the above cliques might notice us in the hall and think, Where did that person come from? Exchange student perhaps? But beyond that, we are invisible. This has enabled us to develop our weird sense of humour. We laugh all the time.

About things that are not funny

to anyone

else.

The Poetry of Texting

Nemiah is not a writer — not even a fan of English class (even though, of course, she always gets an A) — but I have sneakily got her writing some creative things when we text. Which is a lot. The best moment of math class (aside from the bell that sets us free) is when she sends me a cryptic description of the teacher's sad wardrobe choices.

Nem: brown suit from 1967? closet full of mothballs? WTF?!

Gretchen: 1975 for sure. notice lapels. WTF = Way Too Fashionable?

Nem: Whatcha Thinking, Freak?

Gretchen: Why The Faux-pas?

Nem: YES!

It's not just her way of keeping in touch. It's friend-love.

Nem: Mr. Stubbin: missed alarm b/c dreaming of Ms Walker in math again. No shower, hence greasy look

Nem: thoughts, Ms Walker?

Gretchen: Ms W: oh god, here comes the unclean freakshow with another date offer. Someone save me!
Nem: poor Ms W. we should save her.

Does That Mean We Are Exclusive?

I guess so. We don't really hang out with other people.

Sometimes we'll have lunch with Nina Chambers and Leanne Soper, or sit by someone's locker while waiting for class. But Nemiah's the only one I really talk to on the phone. She's the one I count as my BFF. We have a bond, a silent knowledge.

When her mom went on antidepressants last year, I made a batch of cookies for her every week. Which made her cry. Nemiah, I mean. She said no one had ever done anything as nice as that for her.

I didn't believe her — she was always getting presents in the mail from her rich, travelling aunt and uncle. But she never forgot the cookies. She got me a huge cookie recipe book for my birthday, the kind that's filled with photos so delicious you want to lick the page.

Portrait of HIM

He is
blond hair, green eyes — not fake green, but moss — and
dimples on cheeks that beg to be poked with my finger.
He is
soccer team standout, good at physics, which I am not —
our kids will get that from him.
He is
Luke Bremmerman, shy in elementary but not shy now.

How would his sexy arms feel around my waist?

Desperate Times

I still haven't found someone to be my chemistry tutor. Not
like I'm holding auditions, but I've been going through a
mental list of everyone I've ever talked to in this school and
none of them seems like a good choice.

Dragging my feet to the water fountain, hoping the day
will just end so I can crash in bed and forget everything, I
notice a guy coming toward me with a bright blue t-shirt
on. I'm not making this up: it says, I Heart Chemistry, in
white letters. Things start moving in slow motion and a ray
of sunlight hits the words on the shirt (or so it would go in
the movie about my life). I wave my hand like I'm at the
airport meeting a relative. The guy stops and pushes his
thick-rimmed glasses up his nose. Really.

"So are you good at chemistry as well as being a fan of it?" I ask with as much enthusiasm as I can.

"Those two things happen to go together, yes," he says. "Are you?"

"God, no. I hate it." He raises his eyebrows so I rush on. "But I really need a tutor for Chem 11 and your shirt is very convincing. Would you tutor me? I can pay you. It's not a problem."

He glances down at his t-shirt. "I never thought this would be an advertisement. Surreal."

"I know we don't know each other, but it would really, really help me out. Just for a little while. I just need to get my grade up. Please?" I actually clench my hands together under my chin. All-time low.

He adjusts his glasses again.

"Gretchen — is this . . . your tutor?" Of course the tooth fairy is suddenly standing beside me. Of course she's smiling up at both of us.

"Uh, yes?" I say, looking meaningfully at the guy, praying he's astute at seeing desperation in people's eyes. "He's —"

"Going to enjoy reliving Chem 11," he says. "I loved that class."

"Great! James will be a fantastic tutor," the tooth fairy says. "He just won a chemistry competition last month. I'm looking forward to hearing about a better grade, Gretchen."

After she's gone, I turn back to the guy — James. "Thank you for saving me, but what made you say yes?"

He shrugs. "I guess I want to spread the love. Like a chemistry ambassador. A chembassador, if you will."

I smile and nod, thinking I'm not sure I will at all.

Recap of Xmas

Memories of the past holiday season have unfortunately not been blacked out in my brain as I would have liked, and after school today I'll be walking into certain hell: Holiday Photo Album Night.

Mum likes to relive each festive moment by making us fix photos into a new album. We have a bookshelf dedicated to them. Our lives archived forever. Other families use their computers to keep unwanted snapshots hidden. Not us. We print them all out.

Synopsis: my father choked on a walnut at the family Xmas Eve dinner, as we made painful small talk with boring distant relatives. He required Heimliching, and this scared my sister so much she required an early night, so we got to drive home from Port Coquitlam in the pouring rain and got stuck behind a snowplough accident (why was there a snowplough on the road when there was no snow??) and got home grumpy and tired at midnight — technically Christmas day — and fell into bed without brushing teeth. Let's just say, this bad mood and luck with traffic did not improve from then to New Year's. Next year, all

I want for Christmas is to move out on my own, get an apartment and a job, a boyfriend, and not have to spend another torturous holiday season with *them*.

Why I Was Adopted

Of course I wasn't.

I only wish that would explain the weirdness and painful otherness of my family. My father is German, which means: displays of uncalled-for nudity in the house at any time and frequent humming of Bach cantatas when my friends are over.

And lest we forget: the farting.

My mother is Scottish, which means: politeness classes from birth for me and my sister (more on her below), and a formidable collection of wool sweaters.

My chatty, sporty sister, Layla, twelve-going-on-annoying, got cute ringlety pigtails as a child, while I had a bordering-on-boy-bowl-cut. Easy to do the math about that relationship.

Despite the nudity and farting, things are pretty cut and dried:

We must be good, kind little girls,

even if it kills us.

And get As, please.

(Both As and please non-negotiable.)

What I Will (not) Be

if my family has anything to say about it, is a doctor. This is because, since I was four years old and obsessed with playing doctor, I have told them that's what I want to be.

I realized a while ago that a doctor is, in fact, not what I had thought when I was chasing everyone around with my plastic stethoscope. Doctors help people and get to be bossy (the two most alluring things to the four-year-old me), but they also have to deal with people's body fluids and internal organs and work crazy-long hours and be around sick people all day/night.

But by the time I realized that a doctor's life was not for me, my parents had embraced my future career with the enthusiasm of evangelists. I would make the family proud, I would make a ton of money and therefore not need to be worried about. I would meet a nice doctor-man who they would beam with pride about when describing him to their friends. And because this is their dream, I haven't had the courage to tell them it's a lie. They are so happy with the fantasy, and whenever I show them my English grade or a piece of writing, their enthusiasm loses steam. Translation: *That's cute, dear, but writing won't pay your bills or give you a career or make us proud. How's biology going?*

One Thing We Can Agree On

is eating. I am obsessive about many types of food — mostly
due to my family's infatuation with mealtime in general.
Take the amazing crepes we had for breakfast the other
day. Thin and light, stuffed with jam and berries, oh my
god. Wait, isn't that a gospel song?

> *Amazing crepes! How sweet the sound*
> *That saved a wretch like me . . .*

I rest my case.

We think about what to have for dinner as soon as we're
finished breakfast. My friends wonder why I'm not five
hundred pounds and I can only say: good metabolism? But
if they knew what my mum's sister looked like — what my
genetic future could be — they wouldn't be jealous.

Phone Conference at Night

— me to get sympathy/encouragement for my chemistry
grade woes, Nemiah to spring me with news: she's joined
the swim team. She's been swimming on her own for
years, but now she's been to two team practices and says
she's stoked about wearing a latex condom on her head and
spending hours a day in highly chlorinated water.

Apparently her mum wanted to make homemade, spar-
kly signs to hold up at every race. Nemiah managed to talk
her out of that one, and we're both relieved. I try to sound

supportive, even though I'm surprised and a little hurt she's leaving our (miniscule) social circle.

"Gretchen, do you have —"

My little sister barges into my room, unbidden.

I shriek obscenities and she backs out.

"The squirt?" Nemiah asks. She likes Layla, but understands my frustrated older sister viewpoint.

Voices mumble outside my door.

"Better go," I groan. At least if I'm being studious when I get bitched-out it's not as bad.

My Sister's Cuteness

is disgusting. It comes from being the youngest and the prettiest and the one who can't eat anything with soy because it gives her a rash. Revolting.

Here is a haiku about it:

> *Her nasty cuteness*
> *Spoiled little shrimp with freckles*
> *How can she be sister?*

Homework Interruption

As I study virtuously in my room, I am pulled out of an intense article about homelessness by my annoying sibling, who says I have to watch her newest dance routine in the living room with my parents. I decline the invitation but get strong-armed by Dad anyway. I perch (à la tooth fairy) on the couch and watch another five minutes of my life die before me.

The Dance of Idiocy

It begins with the theme from some pre-teen TV show, has a lot of wiggling and flitting of hands, and ends with her on the floor, in a pose that resembles a cat about to puke. I don't say this out loud, but from the look on my parents' faces, I know they don't agree with me.

"Excellent!" my dad shouts; my mum claps along.

"I made up the ending," says my sister, and I half-expect the three of them to group-hug.

"What's the big deal?" I say, and they all look at me like I just shook a baby.

"Gretchen, if you have nothing good to say —"

But I beat them to it. "Thanks for the intermission," I mutter. "Must get back. I have the gentrification of the downtown east side to get through before tomorrow."

I don't see their faces, but I know I've earned a talking-to, and possibly a stare-down at breakfast.

Tutor, Take One

James walks through the radioactive book-thief detectors in the library at exactly three o'clock and sits in the chair beside me like a stick man, as if his arms and legs have no joints, as if he were drawn that way. "Since we haven't actually been introduced," he says, holding out his hand, "I'm James Tarden. Nice to meet you."

"I'm Gretchen Meyers. I really suck at chemistry," I say. "I know you're probably a science genius and I apologize for making you tarnish your chemistry reputation by spoon-feeding it to someone who's hopeless." My pencil tip snaps off.

"I'm not really a spoon-feeder," he says. "And it's pretty depressing to start off hopeless, don't you think?"

I stare at my closed textbook. "Can't get worse than rock-bottom," I mutter.

He holds up a long, skinny finger. "Ah, but I'd argue that rock-bottom assumes there *is* hope. The idea of there being a 'bottom'" — he even makes the air quotes — "indicates that there's nowhere to go but up. Right?"

I stare at him, my stomach at rock-bottom. "Fine."

"But hopelessness is different — it's the absence of hope, which, basically, is death. At least at rock-bottom there's up."

The silence in the library chokes me.

"I'm sorry." James waves his hands in front of him. "I get wrapped up in semantics sometimes. Let's see what you're working on." He opens my textbook and finds the page I dog-eared. He points to the beginning of the chapter enthusiastically. "This totally blew my mind in grade eleven. It's so freaking amazing."

I think: *Well, if you're that stoked, infect me with it, because right now I couldn't care less.* I say: "Ugh."

But he's already skimming the page, reliving his favourite parts. I slouch back in the chair, trying not to stare at the dandruff flaking off his scalp. *He's here to help, he's here to help, he's here to help.*

Help!

2

OH, GOD, I'M A FOODIE

4:35 P.M.

Nem: so??

Gretchen: shoot me now

Nem: don't joke. Library = no place for gun violence

Gretchen: change of subject, movie 2night?

Nem: U can't be in denial about chemistry forever. B 1 w/chem!

Gretchen: denial = coping mechanism. I am coping

Nem: can't. Gotta help mum's boyf move. Shoot ME now

Gretchen: bang bang

Nem: quick, atomic number of gold?

Gretchen: ew, no way

Nem: denial kills!

Gretchen: grenades, rabid dogs, hurricanes, ebola, nuclear war

Nem: ??

Gretchen: things that kill

Nem: fine be that way. Creativity can't save you every time

Gretchen: wanna bet?

At Least There's Lasagna (and Garlic Bread)

My mum's specialty. She may not be Italian, but everyone who's tried it says it's the best lasagna they've ever had. And though it can't take away my cringeful tutoring stint, it helps to soften the memory in a cheesy, garlicky haze.

The Best Way to Spend a Saturday

is NOT to visit the dump with your father, who loves chatting with the guys at the gate and embarrassing you by telling stories of your sordid past as a two-year-old. Seriously — those stories involve eating mud.

But, here I am, stuck with him and bags of garden clippings at the refuse depot. I want to stay in the car but he makes me pull the bags from the trunk while he pays the guy at the booth. Booth-guy is pretty cute, but I think my dad does some guy stare-down thing that says: *Check out my daughter and you'll get a laurel hedge clipping down the throat.* I try my best to walk past his booth, but soon I am summoned to get in the car, and any possible fun evaporates.

The Ride Home

"I wanted to talk to you about Layla," my dad says as we drive back onto the highway. He puts on his sunglasses — the ones that are older than I am and make him look like a bug.

"Am I in trouble?" I ask. Actually I whine it, but who's checking.

He says he just wants to bring something to my attention. I start to worry. I love my sister, I just don't like her, you know?

"She's just going through some changes," he says.

I stare at the sun going behind a high-rise. "Like hormonal?" I ask.

"She's been upset lately that you ignore or make fun of her."

I splutter.

Dad watches the road. "You hurt her feelings when you show contempt."

I pick a leaf off my pants and throw it out the window. "You mean her dancing? Come on — it's hideous."

Dad gives me a stern look. "She's become very sensitive, Gretchen. She's always idolized you. Please be kind."

"Are you serious?"

"She's growing up," he says, not answering my question. "Right now she could use your support."

He looks sad, like he's lost his little girl. I guess he has. Twice. But that's not my fault — it's just puberty. Everyone goes through it. She'll survive.

"Just be kind to her," he says, turning the wheel. "Think about how you'd feel in her place."

Why do they always use that tactic? Other people's shoes. What about my shoes?

Encounter with the Best Kind

The father of my future children
stopped at the water fountain before me,
which means my hand
held the same cold metal his did,
just seconds before.
Note to self: Must try to be less creepy about my crush.

Tutor, Take Two

Tutor James has a huge zit on the end of his nose, and like a beacon, it attracts all eyes within a two-metre radius. What could he have done in a past life to deserve such terrible skin?

"Do you get it?" he asks again, because I am not paying attention.

"So, it's thirty-seven?" I ask.

He asks why. I hate when he asks why.

"I don't know," I moan, and he patiently shows me the formula again.

Focus on the chemistry, focus on the chemistry. The chemistry focus on the —

"— tried laser treatment, but it hurts a lot," he's saying.

What? Did I fall asleep?

"For my skin. It even grosses me out," he says. "I feel bad inflicting the public with it."

I avert my eyes and study the graphic on his t-shirt. It's the periodic table of elements. The whole thing.

"It's a medical condition. Not contagious or anything," he says.

"I wasn't . . . I didn't . . ." I don't know how to finish.

"I just wanted to get it out there, since we'll be sitting here together for a while. It's something people notice." He glances at a pair of preppy-boy Legwarmers walking by us. They smirk together and it's hard to know if that's just part of their general behaviour or directed at our table.

"Sure. Thanks," I say, not sure that I'm sure, or what I'm thanking him for.

Unprovoked

After our lesson, James and I take off in different directions. I head for my locker, salvation in Mum's carrot zucchini muffins. James heads — I know not where.

But halfway down the hall there are shouts of laughter behind me and I can't help turning.

Three rejects are pulling the shirt off some unfortunate kid. His books are strewn across the floor. They're on the lacrosse team, these three known for punching people into lockers if they have an itchy fist.

I'm about to look around for someone of authority when I see who the victim is. A teacher comes out of a classroom and scatters the bullies just as James's t-shirt rips between two of them. James grabs it and takes off shirtless. The teacher heads after the lacrosse guys, barking punishments.

I stand where I am for a long time. The hairs on my arms won't stop prickling.

11:58 A.M.

Gretchen: saddest act of de-t-shirting in the hall just now. I hate bullies
Nem: I hear U. Who was it?
Gretchen: lacrosse idiots
Nem: no, who was de-t-shirted?
Gretchen: don't know. Didn't see their face.

The Cooking Club

I am approached after French by the leader of the cooking club, which calls itself The Foodies. Her name is Ashlyn and we went to elementary together but we haven't talked in years. She swings her blond hair over her shoulder and asks if I want to be part of a worthwhile club, the kind that makes things, really gets involved.

I assume that's the getting-the-hands-floury, rolling-up-the-sleeves part of cooking. Part of me wants to tell her I'm probably more versed in the kitchen than she — food-obsessed as my family is — but then she'd challenge me to duel over cupcakes or something. I bet she thinks I'll bounce right back to the kitchen with her. Does she know her offer sucks?

"We have cinnamon buns," she says.

That might work on a guy but I'm made of tougher stuff. She walks away disappointed — her head actually hangs a little — and I feel bad for putting a dent in her perkiness. Maybe the cooking club wouldn't be so bad.

Later, Nemiah slaps me on the arm when I tell her. "Why didn't you join?" she says. "Free food! You could bring some to the swim team — we're always hungry!"

I shrug it off, a little dented that her "we" didn't include me.

Progress Report

The tooth fairy wants to know how tutoring with James is working out. I pad the truth: problems solved, connections made. She writes in her file folder, saying she'll check back in next week and that Mr. Marchand is overjoyed to hear about James tutoring me.

"I wanted to show you this collection I just picked up." She hands me a thin book with half a picture of a bird on it.

27

It screams poetry. I flip to the table of contents.

This is what I always do — scan the titles of poems for one that stops me. That's the first one I read.

"Her lines are so elegant," she's saying. "I was really impressed that it's her first collection."

I find it: "Mesmer and the Goldfish." That's the first one I'm going to read —

"Gretchen?"

"Huh?"

"I said you should think about writing toward a collection. It takes years, of course, but I know you're really prolific. I can see it now." She smiles in that way adults do when they want to encourage you but not seem too eager.

I close the book. "You can see it now?"

"Sure. Now just work on that chemistry grade so you can relax and spend your time doing what you really want." She taps my shoulder. "Right?"

Clique of One

In the old days, Nemiah and I would be inhaling microwave popcorn and making fun of reality TV stars. We'd be painting her toenails silver and mine chocolate. Now, at home, wondering how Nemiah's swim practices are going, I try to convince myself there are plenty of things to do without resorting to a crutch like the cooking club. I take out a lawn chair and read the book of poems in the sunny garden. But it's February and my fingers are numb in minutes. I practice writing metaphors for kitchen utensils. They all sound like sexual innuendo.

I even break down and do a five-million-piece puzzle with Layla — a cheerful scene including kittens and balls of wool. She likes to laminate each puzzle and hang it on her wall. Isn't that what kids did for fun in the nineteenth century? I call Nemiah and get voicemail.

Leave a message.

Ashlyn's Joy/My Regret

I crumble, call the number beside Rutgard, Ashlyn J. Hold the phone away as she shrieks, tells me to come to the Foods room on Wednesday for the next meeting. Mrs. Fletcher's the teacher supervising, but she's pretty relaxed. Ashlyn thinks this gives them licence to make really out-there things like soufflés and caramel lava cakes. Pride tries to strangle me as she blabs on. Jelly moulds, paring knives, sculptured vegetables. Three-tiered cakes. The only thing I can do is say that I'll be there and hang up.

Screw the First Meeting

Foodies engulf me in the hall Tuesday like I'm a new captive in their little tribe. Fresh meat, if you can pardon the pun. I guess I've found new friends, whether I want them or not.

"Ashlyn says you know a ton about food," one girl says. "Are your parents chefs?"

"No, just European," I say.

"Are you vegetarian? We don't like vegetarians — we want everyone to try everything," another kid says.

"Like tripe and sweetbreads?" I ask, horrified.

The kid looks at me blankly.

One point for Gretchen — these morons don't even know their way around a butchered animal.

I beg off to run for biology, knowing it'll be a long afternoon tomorrow.

4:24 P.M.

Gretchen: cooking club is populated with CRAZY PEOPLE

Nem: crazy-good or ??

Gretchen: definitely ??

Nem: you'll fit right in! JK, you're the sanest person I know. And you love food. You could lead that club

Gretchen: no thanks

Nem: R U and Nemiah hooking up?

Gretchen: ??!

Nem: sorry G! Miles text-jacked my phone! Idiot! TTYL?

Gretchen: who's Miles?

Tutor, Take Three

James and I meet at our table in the library. It is our table now. It has his energy and my confusion etched into its surface. (In fact it says: Jeremy is a male slut; B.R. + S.J.; Love Rules!)

No one dares sit at our table, as if they know when we'll be meeting. I wish I could enter the library, see the tables all filled and say, *Too bad, James, guess we can't meet today.* But that never happens. He is relentless in his desire for me to love chemistry, and I am relentlessly bad at it. Which doesn't mean I'm not getting a slightly better grade — even I will admit some of the stuff is coming more easily — but it's still torture and I still feel like a dunce.

James, nice geek that he is, pulls out my chair and asks me random questions in an effort to ease me into the lesson. For some reason I've told him that my parents want this grade way more than I do. The honesty feels good. Together we give them the nickname "The Board."

James wears obscenely geeky t-shirts every day (the ripped one never appears again) and today it's the chemical structure of something with the words *Sexy, huh?* underneath. He sees me looking at it. "Do you get it?"

"Of course not."

He points to the formula. "It's oxytocin. The 'love' hormone." There are those air quotes again.

"Ah," I say. "Clever."

"Hey, I saw you with the food people," he says.

He knows about the cooking club?

"I think that's cool," he says. "Cooking is actually just chemistry if you think about it."

"Oh, no no — don't turn one of my passions into chemistry. That's depressing." I put my head on the table.

"You have a passion?" He looks at me intensely.

"Well, yeah. I guess a few."

He cocks his head like a spaniel or something.

"My family is food obsessed. We make our own yogurt. I know some cooking terms that impress the food club. It's not that big a deal."

But he's shaking his head. "This is great. We can use this. Glucose, lactose — I can show you the chemical structure of basic molecules in food and how they get denatured and converted by the heating process. It's perfect!" He looks at me so triumphantly that I can't say what I'm thinking: *Doing that will ruin my love for cooking! Why can't we keep the sucky separate from the sublime?*

Nemiah's Invitation

It seems the world of swimming is beyond me — a simple landwalker. Nemiah asks if I'll go to see her swim in her first competition (a swim meet) and be her cheering section. Her mum will be working an extra shift at the pet store she manages. This makes us Sport-and-Entourage, something I never in a million years thought was possible.

"What do I have to do?" I ask. We're walking to her house after school.

"Just be there and scream really loud when I swim," she says. She always wears her hair in a tight ponytail now. It makes her forehead look big but I don't tell her.

"What if you lose?" I ask.

She looks at me funny. "So?"

"Won't you be embarrassed that I was making all that noise?" I would be.

She stares at something behind my head. "Being on a team is about competing, doing your best. It doesn't matter how you finish."

I start to do our gag routine, thinking she's joking, but I realize she's not.

"Will you come?" she asks again.

I wonder if I'll be the only non-swim-related person there. I hug her and her backpack. "Of course I'll come."

Haiku for Licorice

Red twisted threads shine
from the torn bag on my lap
we devour with grins

Oh God, Here Goes Nothing

I am a Foodie. This sucks. It's Wednesday afternoon and I feel like I'm going into an exam. There's nobody I'm friends with here. There are no hot boys in Speedos. No lifeguards.

We better be making something chocolate.

Seven-Layer Dip

Method: take a bunch of yummy ingredients and layer them on a plate. Take some nacho chips and eat the layers. Tasting notes: salty, spicy, creamy — gimme more.

Ashlyn's impressed that I can chop green onions really fast, like a chef. I only cut myself once.

She's so happy I've changed my mind about the club that she's my new best friend. I kind of feel icky about it — she's nice and really helpful, but it's like I'm cheating on Nemiah.

"Next week we're making chocolate mousse," Ashlyn says, washing her hands in the sink for the seventh time.

Just then [angels sing here] LUKE MY LUKE walks into the Foods room and all movement ceases. Well, only mine does. I freeze with what must be a deer-in-the-headlights look on my face. Oh, god, let me not have a zit on my forehead. "Hey," Ashlyn giggles, and sidles over to my future husband. Then the impossible happens. The polar ice caps melt all at once and we are enveloped in a sudden and ferocious flood.

Okay, no. Something worse happens. Luke kisses Ashlyn on the cheek. Ashlyn hugs him with her clean hands around his neck.

I try not to puke up my seven-layer dip.

Haiku for My Loss

How broken, broken
Not a living heart remains
I ache: only Luke

3

DEFINE: GEEK

Tutor, Take Four

James is actually, shockingly, late. After ten minutes of my doodling lightning forks into Ashlyn's head, he drags himself through the door.

"Apologies," he whispers (he is very obedient of library rules).

"What happened?" I ask.

He shakes his head and opens my textbook. "People issues. You don't want to know."

I stick my neck out (figuratively). "Yes, I do."

He shakes his head again. That's a lot of exercise for his scrawny body. "It's unimportant. Let's chemistrate."

"If it's parent issues, I know about that. You'll recall the Doctor Dream? The Board completely doesn't understand me," I say to give him an out.

He snorts. "That can't be correct English."

"And do you tutor English?" I say. "You know what I

mean. They're totally in denial about who I am."

He nods appreciatively. There's a moment when I think he'll say something about his issues, but he thumbs through the textbook and is silent.

"So?" I ask.

He stares at the page. "Let's chemistrate."

Parental Concern

My worried mother (who worries as a pastime, not just sometimes), corners me before dinner the next night to ask if there's something I want to tell her. Do I have any news of good grades? New friends? How's Nemiah? Firstly I tell her to mind her own beeswax (actually I sigh heavily, but it has a waxy feel to it). Secondly, I say, one must not ask so many questions. Questions make one appear foolish. I actually do say this; it gets me a dirty look. Thirdly, I tell her Nemiah's getting along swimmingly (ha!) and that I have to get to my chemistry homework. She smiles faintly, unable to resist this positive attitude.

I win this round.

Layla Asks for a Favour

As I'm drifting off to sleep at eleven, my bedroom door squeaks open.

"Are you asleep?" Layla asks.

Why do people ask this? Why don't they say, "Are you awake?" If I was asleep I wouldn't be answering!

"I'm asleep."

She sits on the bed. I open my eye a slit. She's wearing her Winnie the Pooh nightie and her hair is in a messy ponytail. "I have a date," she says.

In spite of myself I sit bolt upright in bed. "You have a what?"

She looks startled, then giggles. "I'm going to a movie with a boy. And our other friends. But he asked me first."

Her face is red — even in the dark I can tell.

"That doesn't sound like a date," I say.

Her tone is certain. "It's a date."

I take a moment to consider my options:

1. Be the big sister. Offer advice, be cool. Lend her makeup and swear I didn't.

2. Be above grade seven so-called dating. Claim to have no interest and threaten to call the cops (M&D) if she keeps me awake any longer.

She stiffens at a sound outside my door like a deer hearing a hunter in the woods. She's so small, so cute in some ways, it's hard at this moment for me to hate her, even though I do. I want to know who this boy is.

I go for option 1.

She celebrates quietly on my purple throw rug like a freak. I offer to show her some suitable makeup possibilities in the morning.

"What about clothes — what should I wear?"

It's like she's going there tonight.

"Can we wait until tomorrow?" I groan.

Her face falls and I know I could throw down the veto because it's my room, my sleep and my big sister experience she's counting on.

I switch on my bedside lamp.

She gets ready to leap again.

"Just two minutes," I warn.

We spend half an hour looking for tops small enough to fit her bony shoulders.

What This Means

My little sister potentially has a better dating record than mine. I wake up to this thought the next morning, after the warm glow of being the helper of true love wears off. She's only twelve and already she has a date, a movie date, not just a let's-kiss-in-the-woods-behind-the-grade-seven-portable date. Okay, so that wasn't really a date. Unfortunately, that's all I have. It was Kevin Millar and he was supposed to be a veteran kisser. I couldn't tell, being a novice, but it felt wet and warm and not awful, so when he told all his friends I wanted to do other things with him, I naturally freaked out — and said yes. I was the coolest girl in our class for a week — until I realized what "other things" might be. Then I punched Kevin in the gut and got suspended.

So far, Layla's beaten me to a real date and in the harsh morning light it stings a little. I consider taking back the shirt I lent her.

Tutor Is Heavy

James is into heavy metal. Last century, rock-the-spandex-and-long-hair metal. I know because my cousin used to listen to it in his basement and it made me scared of basements until I was ten.

I discover his musical taste when James is actually at our table on time, and I am late. He's wearing his ear buds and doesn't see me, so I yank one out and listen before he can turn the music off. "Hey! What are you doing?" he shouts (the librarian sends us death rays).

"You're a metal head?" I say in a stage whisper. "That's unexpected. It makes you so three-dimensional."

"Because I wasn't before you knew this?"

"No, that's not what I mean. It's an expression."

He looks at me through those terrible glasses. "I want to show you something." He takes out a blank notebook.

"What — you write poetry?" I say. I guess notebooks just push my poetry trigger.

"God, no — only uber-geeks do that," he says, glancing at me with what appears to be a trace of a smile.

"Screw you."

He slaps the table. "So I was right. You are the poetry

geek whose poem is in the hall by the trophy case. Initials GM. I knew it."

I've completely forgotten about that poem. It was from grade nine English, an anonymously entered contest where the students chose the winner. I got Nemiah to take a photo of me next to the case but the glare from the flash makes it hard to read. "So I like poetry — so what? You like chemistry. My neighbour's dog likes toilet water."

He points at something in the notebook. It's a doodled sketch of a slogan, like the ones on his t-shirts. *Geeks: turning enthusiasm into stuff the world needs since forever.*

"Okay, what's with the t-shirts?" I ask. "Was there a sale somewhere?"

"Actually they're pretty expensive." He points to the one he's wearing — a profile of some guy. "It's Becher — phlogiston theory of combustion?"

"You're kidding, right?"

"Okay, so this one's a little obscure. But *this* is going on a t-shirt — I'm getting it made." He points at the slogan in the notebook again. "This is the problem with the social community of high school. No one understands the value of geekdom. How come what I love makes me a geek, but what Henry Gladstone loves makes him a stud?"

"Because Henry Gladstone is a basketball star."

"So? He's a good athlete and he practises a lot and he can spout all the stats from the games. He's skilled and enthusiastic, right?"

I'm starting to get where he's going with this. "You mean, how come being good at something and having enthusiasm makes *him* a god and *you* a geek?"

"Basically, yes."

I look around the library at the people with cool clothes and not-so-cool clothes, the Drama Queens harassing the librarian and the Crunchy Granolas cruising the stacks. "I don't know."

"And what is the opposite of geek? Because it's not what you think it is." He taps his notebook with my pen.

"And what I think is . . . ?"

"That it must *have* an opposite, which it doesn't."

I'm about to ask him if I can just do my chemistry homework tomorrow because I'm kind of scienced out, when he says, "If being a geek means you're intense and skilled at something and love talking about it, then non-geeks are the real losers. Because what does that make them? Uninterested, uninteresting."

I stare at the slogan on his page. "So it's better to be a happy geek than unhappy pretend-cool."

"Right."

"Well, that's too bad," I say.

"Why?"

"Because no one's told the cool people that, and they still rule our world."

Bubble Gum

Since my blissful love fantasy was steamrollered by Luke and Ashlyn, Nemiah's been pretty busy, and I'm starting to wonder if she's avoiding me. I've texted her a few times, but either her phone's broken or she's mad at me. Or something worse.

After English I find her by her locker, popping three sticks of bubble gum at once. Her cheeks bulge.

"You training or something?" I ask.

"Wha?" she mumbles.

"For the bubble-blowing Olympics?" It's stupid but she smiles.

"I haven't seen you in *forever*," she says, "Oh my god, I pulled a muscle in my back so bad."

I nod, unsure how that explains her being MIA.

"You want to come over after school?" I ask.

She winces. "I have to do homework. Tomorrow's the swim meet. Gotta sleep."

I make it sound like that's understandable but it's not — I can't shake the feeling there's something up.

"Hey, Nem." A red-headed girl comes up to us and leans against the lockers. "You psyched about fly?"

I guess this must be some code because Nemiah says, "Yeah, totally."

They giggle and then remember I'm there, and I wish I wasn't, my stomach twisting a little because Nemiah's got a world without me. A secret language.

When

I was in grade three, the new girl in class wore homemade jeans and mismatched socks. She had bangs that were too short and clip-on earrings that she must have taken from her grandmother's jewellery box. The first day, as she stood at the classroom door, her eyes scanned the room for someone who would be her friend. She ate lunch alone for three days until I sat down beside her and we compared sandwich contents.

Me: ham and havarti with cucumbers. Nemiah: peanut butter and jam.

Crying Is Stupid

So I don't cry. I vent.

On Layla.

It's date time.

I'm eye-shadowing her.

L: You think purple?

G: No.

L: Petal pink?

I take it away.

We go for subtle.

Burnt amber.

Her lids shimmer

like a prom queen's.

Venting begins

when she insists
on doing her own
mascara and jerks
the wand
from my hand.
She's like a goddamn
toddler.
Can't she see
I know what I'm doing?
I snap, poke her
in the forehead
with it, dark
smear hole,
tears and howling.
I guess I deserve
the death threat
my mother gives me.

On Your Mark!

I sit in the highest row of the chlorine-infused bleachers
and wait to recognize my best friend's freshly shaved legs
walk out of the women's change room.

I am beside a mother and her preschooler, who slurps a
yogurt drink and keeps looking at me like I'm some kind of
family member. I forgot how happy four-year-olds can be.

Then the audience claps and the teams march out, and

there's Nemiah, my pride and joy, even though I couldn't get a hold of her to say good luck. She looks into the crowd and waves; I wave back, as does half the audience. I feel like a giddy loser.

The preschooler laughs. Soon the swimmers have disrobed and each lane has an antsy, swim-capped competitor waiting to dive into it. Nemiah's all focus. I try to stare hard enough that she'll look at me, but she rubs her legs and stares at the clock. I inhale warm chlorine air and clap as the first race ends with a tie by two brothers.

Finally it's her turn and I find myself on my feet, heart beating for her, praying she doesn't mess up, and I remember what she said: it doesn't matter if she wins, just that she swims. At this moment there is no more profound statement. I scream as she swims the final length, so strong, so athletic.

I cheer with the four-year-old as the race is won by a girl from another school. Nemiah comes in third. I couldn't be prouder; I want to high-five everyone.

After Party

Nemiah wet-hugs me as I make my way down after the meet. She shrieks in my ear but I don't mind losing a little hearing.

"You came! Wasn't it awesome?" She doesn't seem to need a response. "You have to come with us!"

"What's going on?" I ask, and Redhead Girl from the locker says, "Party at Becca's. There's always lots to see."

I don't know what that means, but I giggle with them.

"What do you guys do?" I ask.

Apparently that's a stupid thing to say: Red rolls her eyes, saying, "God, nothing crazy, we carbo load and jump on the tramp."

This must be the best thing about being an elite athlete. You get to party after with your teammates and other hot people.

"You should come," Nemiah says. "Shay's mum can give you a ride." Shay (Red) shrugs her assent and I am officially a third wheel.

4

DROWNING

Haiku: Swim Team Party

Svelte bodies jumping
to Moroccan hip-hop beats
They gorge on penne

What Happens at These Things

Now I know, as one of the initiated, that swim team parties
are the weirdest things invented. They occur after the meet,
during the day, there is no alcohol (visible to the naked
eye) and no weed (once again . . .) and everyone is SO
DAMN HAPPY and devours plates of noodles. There really
is a trampoline, but it's called a tramp because Becca's sister
is an elite gymnast and in the biz it's called a tramp —
like *skank* for my mum's generation. They jump and jump.
No one pukes up their pasta. These people are machines.
Front-crawling, giggling, iron-stomached machines.

Nemiah has left me in the middle of the lawn and taken off with Shay and a few other swim girlies, and I stand there like a tree waiting for her to realize she forgot me. I imitate cedar and Douglas fir for ten minutes. Then maple for ten minutes more.

This Is Stupid

I know I look like a fool.

A foolish tree.

People brush past me, trying not to stare. How could she leave me here? Bitterness rises in my stomach and I make a move. To the bathroom.

I can think in there, on the toilet with the lid down. It's fuzzy pink. Okay, breathe.

I have to find Nemiah. She's probably looking for me.

Shut Down

In the kitchen, Shay's filling balloons with water. Aha.

"Is there a battle?" I ask, trying to sound casual.

She glances my way and shrugs. "If you say so."

"Those — are you going to throw them?"

She ties one off. "That's what they're *usually* used for."

I can tell I'm a noxious underground insect to Shay, but I dig myself a little deeper.

"Do you know where Nemiah is?"

Shay puts the water balloons in a tub and walks toward the deck. "At this second? Not sure."

I follow, waiting long enough that I look like I'm not following. I fail.

Shay turns and gives me a look that hisses *don't follow me*.

I glance around. This is about as much female hostility as I can take in a day. I feel a little shaky. Nowhere do I glimpse Nemiah's long, dark ponytail. It's all I want to see in the world.

Finally I Spot Her

by the rhododendrons,
crouching with other girls
like they're hiding.
Something flashes past
and splooshes water —
a balloon. Shay runs to them
with her ammo,
squealing. She says something
to Nemiah, handing her
a balloon. I watch, waiting
for her to get up, leave
the fun and games
and tell me it's stupid,
she's going home with me
to hang out, just us.

But she looks at me
for a second, back at Shay,
and back at me, motioning
with her hand. "Come here,"
she mouths. Shay's busy
fighting the good fight.
My gut drops. She'll never
believe me if I tell her
how bitchy Shay was.
I wait one more
second, but a water bomb
hits her on the head,
and she shrieks, grabbing
at Shay to get out
of firing range.

I take two clumsy
steps backwards.
Then another, and
another.
Soon I've walked
all the way down
the driveway
and onto the road.

After Effects

My ears ring like I've been at a concert.
Did that just happen?
I feel hazy, a little dizzy.
I walk down the cul-de-sac, where the grade twelves'
cars are parked, all shiny and borrowed,
along the sidewalk.

Long Road Home

I wander the neighbourhood looking for a bus stop and thinking how Nemiah's new friends will all glare at me on Monday. I don't care. She left me.

She left *me*. I'm officially pissed off and hurt.

I stomp out onto a main road and try to find a landmark I recognize. All strange houses, strange cars, nothing I know — damn, I should have asked where the hell we were. Finally a bus comes by and I race ahead of it, looking for the bus stop. Guess who gets there first?

I sit at the bus stop for half an hour. An old man plunks down next to me. He smells overwhelmingly like cat food.

Right now I'd even take Layla for conversation.

I call home on my cell, but there's no answer so I sit there and try not to smell cat-food-man or get gunk on my jeans from the bench.

I get home two hours after I left the party. Naturally, my parents were out shopping until just before I got there.

My mum questions me lightly, but I don't give much away. She asks if I want to help make a trifle for a dinner party they're going to. I like custard and cake, so I say okay, but I feel like a kid who's left out of the playgroup and is placated by the grown-up with some unimportant job. Placing slices of banana between custard and brandy-soaked cake.

Recipe for a Mother-Daughter Relationship

Ingredients:

    One controlling mother

    One strong-willed daughter

    Detailed history

    A sprinkle of hormones

    A lot of tension

    A few misunderstandings

Directions:

Marinate the first two ingredients in the history for sixteen years. Sprinkle in the hormones and tension and watch the mixture bubble up. Stir in a few misunderstandings. Pour everything into a pan and bake in a 350-degree oven for as long as you can stand it. After a while, you'll have a hot mess that will continue developing flavour the longer you leave it.

Haiku: Cereal

Crunch like breakfast bones
milky morning spoon droplets
time makes things soggy

And here's a real one that kind of cheers me up. Kind of.

First winter rain —
even the monkey
seems to want a raincoat.
— Bashō

The Update on the Date

I forgot with all my own drama that my sister is dating a grade seven boy. His name is Wes (no last name apparently) and he took her to see a romantic comedy and they ate popcorn and held hands. Yes, they had a gaggle of friends around them, but still — I'd kill for any of those scenarios right now.

She arrived home at nine-thirty-two, a smile stretched across her face, her makeup still pristine, and my mum gave her a hug that meant both *My baby's growing up!* and *You're two minutes after curfew!*

I watched from the couch and finally she sat down beside me. "Thanks for your help," she said.

"Did he kiss you?" I prodded.

She stared at the TV as it flashed.

"Did he?"

She blinked in that satisfied way a python does when it's digesting a baby warthog. She squeezed my hand. "I'm in love," she said. And even though I knew in my cynical, older-sister mind that this was not love, I squeezed back.

The Politics of Friendship

Here is how I see it:

Nemiah should call me. I did nothing wrong, nothing any normal jilted person wouldn't do, walking out of a party that wants to eject me anyway. It's up to her to apologize.

Here's how the rest of my weekend went:

No phone ringing. No knock on the door, no paper airplanes through my window. Only Layla practising her revolting dances and swooning about Wes, and my parents talking about Middle East struggles and what to have for dinner.

Here's what I expect at school:

She'll come up to me, maybe a little awkwardly at first, and say she's sorry for not being a better friend at the party and can we hang out, just the two of us, after school? We'll talk about boys and our least favourite classes and buy licorice on the way home.

What Really Happens

She ignores me.

Flat out and completely. She is flanked by her new posse — Shay in pole position. They breeze by me in the hall, and I'm embarrassed to admit my mouth hangs open for a few seconds after they pass. Time stops.

My lungs are empty and I can't fill them.

What just happened?

She's my sister-in-life, my best friend, my rock in this hell we call school. And I'm dead to her?

I rush to the washroom and sit in the nearest stall, waiting to wake up.

Was I wrong not to call her?

Should I be the one to apologize?

Why do I always end up sitting on the toilet?

My hands are cold and I rub them on my jeans. I know I have a class to get to, but I can't remember what it is.

"Gretchen?"

I spy unfamiliar sneakers under the stall door. I get up and walk out into the cruel world. It's Ashlyn. All blond and flower-print-collared-shirt. She looks concerned.

I Have a Half-Friend

and I feel like the biggest loser in school. Everyone Nemiah and I ever talked to knows that we're not talking (why

aren't we talking?!) and they all have a side. Unfortunately, most side with the swim team — they're cuter. Nina
Chambers and Leanne Soper conveniently become invisible whenever I walk down the hall. I guess that puts them
in the opposing corner, or at least neutral, which for me is
just as bad.

Ashlyn becomes my personal crutch for the day. For
some reason she stayed with me in the bathroom until the
second bell rang and I was late for class. She finds me at
lunch and offers me her yogurt.

"I just know what girls can be like," she says, as if she's
beyond us all. Then she smilingly adds, almost as an after-
thought, "You're helping with the banquet later, right?"

Slave Labour at the Banquet

This day has passed like a dream — no, a nightmare — and
I can't believe I'm scooping hummus into glass bowls rest-
ing on doilies of which my grandmother would be proud.

I have been socially coerced into labouring as a server
for the badminton team's victory dinner. I need Ashlyn,
I realize, if I am to save any kind of reputation from this
mess I'm in. Her Blondness smiles at me from across the
gym, where she serves punch and giggles with skinny-cute
Asian boys on the team.

Everyone knows I am humiliated. Everyone knows I am
alone. I just don't know *why*. I call my house on my two

minute break and explain why I'm not home yet. They're pumped that I'm helping.

As the badminton team finally wanders off school grounds to find a better party, we begin to clean up. Ashlyn gets me stacking paper plates smeared with dinner remnants. After a minute I duck under the tablecloth when no one's looking and stay there until a stupid grade nine rips the cloth off and reveals my cave.

I don't get offered a ride home.

5

DELI MEETS

Did I Mention Layla's Boyfriend?

He's a hockey player. He eats wheat germ muffins and his mother is a yoga instructor.

Layla tells me this the morning after I've spent all night by the phone waiting for Nemiah to call. (More on the depression, anger and bitterness later.)

She announces that they like the same *everything* — music, sports drinks, cereal, blah blah blah. I want to choke on my toast and disrupt the bliss of the moment: my cute sister smiling through her Cheerios, her hair shiny and her pink t-shirt mocking my pyjamas.

"Why aren't you dressed?" my mum asks me.

"I think she's depressed," says my concerned sister.

Their rhyming forces me to bolt to my room.

Phone Call Prose Poem

After three false tries, a huge lump in my throat, I call Nemiah the next morning. It's early, barely eight. She doesn't have swimming on Tuesdays. Leaking through my wall is the sound of Layla butchering a pop song. I thump the wall but she doesn't hear me. Nemiah's phone rings and rings. I count eight, nine, ten. *Pick up pick up pick up.* "Yello?" It's her mum. "Hi, Ms Hershey," I say. "Is Nemiah home?" Her phone's being switched to the other ear. "Well, hey, Gretchen. No, she's gone. She said you might call." "She did?" Nemiah's mum clears her throat. "Yeah, some nonsense about you guys having a fight. You okay?" The tears prickle the back of my eyes and I will them not to show in my voice. "I'm fine. I guess I'll see her at school." There's a radio crackling in their kitchen. "She's been acting strange, Gretchen, ever since the weekend — don't know why." I want to ask her about it, what Nemiah's told her mum, but my voice will crack. "I better go," I say. "Thanks." The numbness in my hands creeps up my arms as I put the phone down. Layla has turned off her music. The silence kills me, and I wish it was still blasting so I could be drowned out — stupid, useless person that I am, friend of no one.

Humiliation Before Brains

Something comes over me halfway through math — a whim of stupidity, desperation — and I text Nemiah, who has cozied up to a girl from the swim team: beige hair, too much eyeliner.

Nemiah hears her phone beep, I know it, but pretends not to, and it sticks out of her bag for twenty minutes as I use my ESP to make her check it.

Finally she does, just as Mr. Stubbin asks if there are any questions about the homework. Someone in the back asks something stupid and Mr. Stubbin drones out an answer.

Nemiah reads the text, shows it to eyeliner girl, and they giggle together as the bell rings.

Scrape of chairs, thunder of feet and chatter of voices. I am frozen in my seat. I wonder what part they were laughing at: the part that pleads for her to meet me after school to talk, or the part that says she's still my best friend.

Lesson Rejection

I really
really don't feel like
dealing with chemistry,
but James is there
when I get to the library.
His green t-shirt reads
Thank God for Science!

and this time I have no patience

for his sense of humour.

I slouch.

He opens my textbook

for me, because all

I can do is stare blankly

at the table.

"You okay?" he asks.

I shrug. "Yeah, why?"

"You seem down."

"I'm fine."

"I heard —" he starts,

then stops.

"I'm sure you did," I say.

He closes my textbook.

"Screw this.

Let's get out of here.

I'm done with this place."

Deli-cious

We go to Carter's Deli, which is owned by James's uncle.
I've never heard of it, even though it's not far from my
neighbourhood, but it's amazing. It rocks fifties counters
and black and white lino. We sit by the window with subs
packed with meat. I feel like a guy.

James jokes with his cousin, who's eighteen, works here,

also not my type. But they're both nice. It feels easy.

They both have brown shaggy hair and bad acne, except Cousin's is healing. Cousin has a long gangly frame like James's, but it has filled out some — maybe there's hope. Cousin has a good smile, deep blue eyes unframed by glasses. The two of them joke about working in a deli, being cousins, Star Wars, which is Cousin's obsession — "Sci-fi in general, but Lucas's films in particular," James informs me. I look at him more closely as he laughs. He never laughs at school. It suits him.

After an hour, it starts to rain and I wonder if I should call a parent. "I'm off now," Cousin says. "You guys want a ride?" His actual name is Dean. (Jokes about James Dean plagued their childhoods. And they're surprised I know who James Dean is. "Come on," I say to their obvious approval, "he's classic.")

We hop in Dean's clunky hatchback, Lucy, the smell of french fries rising from the seats. I don't care — I'm having fun. I've even (almost) forgotten about Nemiah. We butcher rock songs as we drive (mandatory singing in Dean's car due to his broken stereo).

He glances at me (riding shotgun) and chuckles. "You're one of the boys now, Gretchen. Sure you can handle it?"

"She can handle it," James says behind me. "She's pretty hardcore. She knows how to butcher a whole pig."

I whip my head around to see him grinning. "That's such a lie! Where did you hear that?"

He shrugs. "Made it up. But it's based on hearsay I over-heard outside the Foods room. Is it even remotely possible?"

"It does put you in a whole new light," Dean says. "Like maybe you're this fly-by-night butcher girl who has a thing for kidnapping older guys. Whatcha think, James?"

"But I'm not driving," I point out. "And there's absolutely no truth to that pig thing. Who even does that?"

"A butcher," James/Dean say together.

And Then

Before I know it, we've hung out three days in a week.

It's always a blast. James becomes this witty, kind-of-shy, kind-of-silly guy who makes inexcusably cheesy science jokes ("If you're not part of the solution, you're part of the precipitate!") but listens, really listens, to whoever is talking. It makes you feel like you're the most important person at that moment.

Dean is loud, funny and always opening the door for me, even when James teases him about it. Dean has Star Wars ringtones on his phone and has a light sabre tattooed on the inside of his index finger. He shows his affection for James by pushing him into the road — when there are no cars coming. It's actually a lot sweeter than it sounds.

I forget about the soul-crushing loneliness of last week and live in James/Dean world.

It's always sunny here.

Until

We are driving to the beach to see which one of them is man enough to swim in the ocean in winter. Dean repeats his challenge — ten seconds, total body immersion, no wet suits, no crying.

James looks nervous. I try to catch his gaze, to show him it's no big deal to back out, but he stares out the window.

"So what's the prize for the winner?" I ask.

"Other than bragging rights?" Dean says. "Maybe a kiss from the lady. Isn't that how it used to be done?"

"Aw, man, don't do that." James groans. "Are you introducing sexual tension into our group just when it was getting great? That licks."

I must look stunned because Dean drops his jaw and winks at me. "You're cute," he murmurs. "No, I'm not sabotaging the group, James. It's the group above all else, right?"

James says nothing. I am paralyzed, brain frozen. Awkward silence.

"But hypothetically, Gretchen —"

"Stop talking, stop talking, la la la!" James yells from the back seat.

"Okay, fine. We're here anyway. But let me know what you think — you know — when you've thought about it," Dean says to me, leaning in as he unclips his seat belt.

"Sure," I manage to say, but I'm still stuck on the kiss part. Dean wants me to kiss him.

Why does that make the world stop?

And Now What?

After the shock wears off, I start to think about what this means. Does Dean actually want to date me, or is he just teasing me in that pull-your-pigtails kind of way we are always told guys do? And what do I want? Sure, a high school grad for a boyfriend is up there on my list of Coolness I Will Never Hope to Achieve, but do I want to date Dean? What about the friendship we have — and James? We were just getting such a cool vibe, the three of us. I can't afford to mess that up, what with my recent friend track record.

But Dean

decides it all for me. Tuesday afternoon he picks me and James up from the corner outside school. He looks the same as always but my stomach is churning, so exactly nothing is the same. I hate that.

I'm thinking about what to say that will simultaneously let him down easy and not be awkward, when he says, "Hey, Gretchen, about the kiss thing the other day."

I only stare, trying to look unflustered.

"I was totally kidding, okay? It's not like that with us and I respect that. We're buddies. Let's keep it that way."

He glances quickly into the rear-view and I know he's looking at James.

"I wasn't weirded out," I say. "It's no problem," relief and disappointment flooding through me.

"Okay, I need a serious dose of caffeine, people," James says from behind me. "Beeline it for Starbucks, driver."

52 Percent

Upside to this latest chemistry quiz: I actually passed.
Downside: It won't be good enough for The Board.
Does it count if it's good enough for me?

Mum's Thoughts on Life

resemble fairy tales on acid. She thinks I should send Nemiah a letter and all will magically be well. Since she only knows we had a fight and not that I am Ostracized Girl at school, I can't really protest. I peel potatoes into the sink as my duty to dinner while she regales me with her opinion.

"Maybe I should phone her mother," she says.

"Don't you dare!" I wave a naked potato to make my point stronger. "You *can't* help."

Layla waltzes in, peering at us hopefully. "What're you talking about?"

"Nothing," Mum says. "Get to your homework."

Layla looks insulted but takes off.

I finish the spuds and make my escape.

"Wait, Gretchen."

I freeze in hopes Mum can't see me. Works for rabbits.

She unstacks plates. "I miss our chats," she murmurs.

"We used to be so close."

Yeah, I think, *when you still changed my diapers. And before you decided my future for me.*

"Let's have dinner, just us. Maybe next week," she says.

I say I'll think about it, knowing she expects a yes. Knowing the conversation would be awkward and I'll end up angry but unable to say anything.

Knowing I've cut her somehow.

> **Approaching my village:**
> *Don't know about the people,*
> *but all the scarecrows*
> *are crooked.*
>   – Issa

At Times Like This

I forget I once lusted after Luke Bremmerman at all. I swear he's not as cute as I thought — what's with the almost-mullet? Ashlyn, who still clings to my cooking skills ("You're better than everyone combined!"), can have him. Her roots are growing out dark, but she has been pretty nice to me since I became a loser. She says hi to me in the hall as others look on in pity or malice. I have noted that when Luke visits her in the Foods room, he only comes when he can snarf some baking. Yes, Luke and Ashlyn sitting in a tree, I swear to god that's fine with me.

Nemiah Leaves a Message

Heart in throat —
can she be ready
to say sorry, will I
wake up in her room
after a sleepover
and it's all a bad dream —
everything's okay?

I turn up the volume
on the phone
to make sure
I don't miss anything.

"Hey, Mrs. Meyers,
it's Nemiah, I just
wanted to ask if
my yellow jacket is
at your place. I think
I might have left it there
before Christmas.
If so, could you
leave it on the porch?
I'll grab it
tomorrow. Tha—"

I erase the message

halfway through
her thanks.

Five seconds later
I wonder if she
said anything about me
in the part I erased.
Damn.
I throw the phone
on the floor,
but I'm too wimpy
to break it.

6

POETRY WHAT?

Bake Sale Brownies

Ashlyn announces we will make her favourite food in the entire world, ever, on Wednesday, as the cooking club gathers around her like kids to the kindergarten teacher. She revels.

Garth, a puny kid in grade nine who, it's rumoured, eats, sleeps and breathes Dungeons and Dragons, takes the chair next to me. (The rumour goes he wants to change his name to Thor.) At least he's okay in the kitchen. These days my criteria for suitable acquaintances has gone out the window. Garth/Thor makes a joke about what's really in the brownies. A couple of innocents stare blankly.

"We're practising these white chocolate–cherry brownies because I have a surprise for you." Ashlyn giggles. Garth/Thor and I groan in unison and instantly feel a bond. "We're going to have a stall at the Spring Fair!"

I look around at all the empty expressions and Ashlyn

maniacally grinning. "What the hell's that?" I ask. There are grunts of agreement around the room; I feel the power.

Ashlyn looks shocked. "The Spring Fair? Fundraising for the senior class trip? Games, rides, food, fun for all ages? Ring any bells?"

Garth/Thor pipes up. "Why should we slave for them?" More grunts, a few table-slaps. Ashlyn's kindergarten class has officially rebelled.

"We give them a cut of the profits, they're buying the ingredients," Ashlyn explains. We're not buying her logic. "It's a partnership. We can use the money to get new equipment — or go on a field trip!"

I put my hand up. "Well, at least we get in free, right?" I step forward. "I'll sell stuff if we get to take turns on the rides and games." I look around and realize I could take over as leader of the pack (who knew?). "We deserve a reward for our brownies." The cheers around me feel like warm honey — well, not really, but they feel good.

For the Record

Popularity (at school): nil
Popularity (outside school): minimal but respectable
Boyfriend status: nil, but nobody's perfect
Chemistry grade status: la la la, I can't hear you
Hope for the future: faint but growing

Me and My Boys

We are solid, easy, fresh air in a stuffy room, and hilarious — no one makes us laugh like we do.

Dean makes me a playlist that spells out words by the first letter of the song's titles:

Come On with Me, The Crones

Rich Enough, Betty and George

Allison, The Games

Shut Up, The Cosmic Turkeys

How Are You?, Tender Flesh

Not Now, Not Ever, Call Me Crazy

Beautiful, Rock Paper Scissors

Underneath It All, Flavour

Reach Me, Stanley Shepard

Noodles, Not The One You Want

I try not to read into it.

Hint of Spring

The rain lets up for a day and we get the most beautiful, almost-warm morning, on which I walk to school feeling like maybe things will be okay. Maybe I don't need Nemiah.

I consider asking Ashlyn if she wants to go for coffee sometime. She's been looking low lately — it's going around that she and Luke are having issues.

A squirrel runs across the road toward me and stops, chewing a nut.

I pick up an acorn and throw it to him. He scampers off, but a minute later, when I look back, he grabs the one I threw and zips up a tree.

Layla's Agony

She's been dumped. I won't say I expected marriage or anything, but at least it could have lasted a month. I guess grade seven doesn't work like that. She got 3.2 weeks and four sort-of-dates, but one doesn't count because it was a walk home from school.

She sits at the breakfast table and moans about heart-ache and loss. I want to shake her and say, "You don't know squat about those things — try losing your best friend!" but I don't; Mum's at the sink trying not to offer advice.

Layla slumps off to school and, on the order of our mother, I catch her up in the driveway and try for something cheery: "I'll watch that music show with you tonight."

She looks ready to cry. "That was Wes's favourite show!" Gag-fest. She sniffs. "Can you paint my toenails for me?" I wonder what would happen if I answer literally. (Technically? Yes. Do I want to? No.).

"Yeah, all right," I say, and she looks at me gratefully.

I am Super Sister.

Haiku for James
(because he deserves one)

Lanky wrong jeans boy
Exhales smarts like fog on glass
Has the coolest laugh

Run-in with the Tooth Fairy

She finds me in the hall when I least expect it — think fast.
Hard to do at 8:14.

"How are you doing with James?" she asks, all smiles. I
try to smile back as I tell her that I think I'm getting it.

She nods, murmuring about Mr. Marchand knowing his star chemistry student can tutor anyone out of
a black hole. Then she asks excitedly, "Did you read the
poems?"

I dive into the security of poesy and feel much safer. "I'm
really jealous of her sexy line breaks," I say. "And there was
this one image —"

"The frog in the pond?" Her face lights up.

"Yes!"

"Wasn't that gorgeous? I almost cried. And the way it
connected back to her mother . . ." She looks like she's
going to swoon.

"Are you okay?" I ask.

She straightens up. "I'm okay. Oh, and she's going to be
at a poetry slam next month, if you want to check her out."

"Poetry what?" I've never heard of this before, but just the sound of it makes me think I'll love it and be embarrassed by it at the same time.

"It's a performance poetry contest on Commercial Drive. Every Monday." She looks at me from under her thick bangs. "You'd love it, Gretchen. Maybe you could go with James."

"James isn't into poetry — and we're not together." I don't know why I have to say this — we are friends and I could totally ask him and Dean to go with me. "I just don't know if performing poetry is my thing."

"You don't have to perform anything," she says. "Just go and watch. It's poetry that will blow your mind." She unperches herself and turns to go. "And keep up the chemistry work, right?

When I'm Hanging Out

with James/Dean I get to be myself.
Not the me who orders and cooks and cleans messes
in the Foods room. Not the me who
doesn't upset the apple cart at home.
The fun me who howls with the boys
driving down the boulevard,
watching people watch us go by,
wondering how much they want to be us.
I was on the outside once too.

Funny Dean

If I could bronze a moment
like my mum
bronzed my baby shoes,
it would be this:

Dean accidentally walking
through a tai chi session
in the park
on the way
to find ice cream.

Dean purposefully
joining in,
striking a praying mantis
pose beside
an old man whose eyes
were closed.

James and I hiding
behind a bush, stuffing
our hands
in our mouths
to keep from laughing.

The old man
opening his eyes,

seeing Dean in
Tortured Locust position
with his eyes closed,
and shouting so loud
Dean falls over.

I have never
laughed and run
so hard in my life.

An Almost-Glance

I walk down the hall on the way to social studies and it
happens: Nemiah looks up from reading something at her
locker, and maybe she forgets for a second that we are not
talking. She catches my eye and smiles. But then the light
goes on: She's supposed to be a bitch to me. She reverses
the smile and looks away. It's like I can hear the commen-
tary her brain is making to her face muscles: "Cheeks up,
smiling — wait! Abort! Target is not worthy of this reaction! Cheeks down, down! Avert eyes, commence Ignore
Mode!"

I Suggest a Slam

We're sitting in the library — one of the rare times these
days when we actually act like tutor and tutee — and I'm

looking for yet another way to avoid looking at chemical reaction formulas. James is wearing a t-shirt that says *Geeks Rule the World*, and has pictures of Stephen Hawking, Bill Gates and Mark Zuckerberg.

"So, there's this thing next Monday over on the Drive. I kind of want to go and I thought you and Dean might . . ." I don't know how to end. Like it? Save me from myself?

"Define 'thing,'" James says, his finger still on the formula for ammonium sulfide, "because Commercial Drive has a lot of them."

"It's a poetry slam," I whisper.

"What? Speak up. The oppressive silence of the library is drowning you out." His eyes crinkle in the corners. "Did I hear poetry?"

"Slam, yes. It's this performance thing. Like spoken word, but there's judges and winners."

He slaps the table. The sound reverberates around the library like a gunshot. "You, Gretchen Meyers, are a poetry geek. Congrats on the arcane terminology. I have no idea what you just said. It's awesome."

I'm mortified, but I manage to ask if he'll come.

He taps my shoulder lightly. "Hey, don't take it personally. Embrace it. It's your thing. Dean works that night, but I would like to be confounded and confused by a bunch of hopped-up poets on Monday. Count me in."

Unfortunately

Things don't start off well for my first poetry slam. James doesn't show at school on Monday, calls me at lunch to say he's got the flu — so sorry not to witness me in my geek element.

Having made the stupid mistake of telling my parents about the poetry slam (*I'm going with a friend — a real one — you'll be so proud*), I explain that I won't be going anymore. Mum then decides it's her job to fill the James-shaped hole in the evening, likely because I still haven't agreed to go for dinner with her. I can't think of the right thing to say to turn her down. It's actually nice of her to take an interest, considering it's not doctor-related.

But as we pull up to the place, all I want to do is go home. I'm here with my mother. She won't understand what's going on — on several levels. She is wearing a sweater from the year I was born. What was I thinking?

The Scene

We get a small table at the back of the café. Mum orders us hot chocolates and I try not to bolt for the door. Everyone is older than me, cooler than me, and completely without a parent.

"This should be interesting," Mum says as she slides into her chair. "I'm so glad you invited me."

I didn't. You invited yourself.

My heart is racing for some inexplicable reason. The lights dim slightly and the emcee gets up on the little stage.

One Hour and Five Minutes

later, after poets have stood up and read their stuff and the audience has sent the best ones to the final round, a guy with long hair and a goatee wins the slam and the crowd cheers. He deserved it. They all did. I want them all to go again — I want to live this hour again.

I'm not one for competition. Sports are not my thing, but poetry sports — now there's something worthwhile.

I could be an elite poetry athlete.

The Point

I'm buzzed with the energy of the slam as we leave the café — the rhythms and voices and goosebump-inducing lines. It feels like home. This is where I want to be. I want to live here and make all these people my friends.

We walk back to the car in the cold drizzle and I forget my mum is walking beside me, I'm so pumped. I can't wait to get to my room to write. It feels like my brain is cracked open and all the creative ideas I'll ever be capable of are ready to be captured.

"Well, that was different," my mother says. "I'm not sure I understood most of it, but they certainly had a lot of enthusiasm, didn't they?"

I open the passenger door. "I thought it was amazing. I think it was one of the best nights of my life."

She starts the car. "Well, I'm glad you had a good time."

"No, I mean, I want to do that. I want to be a poet."

There it is. Can't take it back now.

"It could be a great hobby, Gretchen. I admire you for being so creative."

"What if I don't want it to be just a hobby?" I stare out the window at the wet streets, my heart hammering.

She pauses. "Well, I don't think there are many poets who write for a living, sweetie. It's not the kind of job that pays the bills. But once you get a practical training, something reliable, you can do something like this slam for fun. We'd love to come and cheer you on."

"You totally don't get it," I mutter.

"What's that?" she asks, distracted by a slow pedestrian.

"Nothing." I say. "Forget it."

And between merging onto the highway and some story on the radio, she does.

Muse

I push aside the conversation in the car — put it in its own box and lock it — and write until one in the morning, until my eyelids feel like sandpaper and I can't make sense of the words.

It feels
more like living
than the living
I've been doing
so far.

By Way of Apology

for missing the slam but also, I suspect, because he can't
help himself, James presents me with a baby blue t-shirt,
folded up neatly on our table in the library.

"Go ahead," he says, grinning and nudging it.

I slowly unfold the fabric, terrified I'll be forced because
of friendship to wear a *Geeks Rule the World* t-shirt. But
instead I find PoEM written as elements from the periodic
table: Po (Polonium) + E (Einsteinium) + M (Muriaticum).

"Wow," I say. "It's . . . not something I ever thought I'd
see."

"I had to fudge it a little — the E and M are older element
names. Don't tell Mr. Marchand." He looks at me. "Do you
like it?"

I stare at the letters — the word, something I love so
much, and the language, something I've always hated —
and I do like it.

Not just because it's creative and weird and random but
because James gets me in a way I never thought he would.

Departure

As we finish the lesson, my homework perfect and mostly understood, James looks suddenly uneasy. His face shuts down, gaze to the floor.

Behind the closed glass library doors, two lacrosse guys make rude gestures in our direction.

"What's the deal with them, anyway?" I go for casual, as if I have no idea.

"I made them look stupid in class last year and they haven't forgotten. Maybe if I was in a gang of Scientist Ultimate Fighters I could level the field." He shrugs and takes a long time closing his bag.

"But you don't have to take it," I say. "There's stuff you can do — people who handle this stuff all the time."

"Yeah, I know. I've explored the avenues."

"Have you?" I glance back at the doors but the guys are gone.

Front-Seat Driver

We cruise in Lucy, Dean and James providing beatbox rhythms as I lay lines from Ezra Pound poems over top.

Dean smiles at me, keeps nodding as I add another line, think of a new poem when the last one ends.

"Where to, lady?" he asks as we come to an intersection.

"Um . . . a washroom? I need to piss," James says from behind me.

"Ah, but you are not the lady, James." Dean winks at me.

"The park," I say. "Port-o-potty for James and swings for me."

"Swings. Executive." Dean puts on his indicator.

They ask for another poem.

Newsflash

If I didn't know better I'd say I've developed a crush on Dean. But I know better. Otherwise I'd want to touch him and not get out of the car when he drops me off. And I'd want to see him smile so much, I'd tell any stupid joke I could think of. But I'm not doing that.

7

CRUSHING

Grrrl

We're at the gas station, waiting for James to finish filling up the tank, when Dean leans over and whispers in my ear: "Let's take off, right now, just you and me." I freeze in my seat. This kind of comment makes me weak, now that I know I'm crushing on him.

I watch James rock out to some tune in his head as he holds the pump. He's such a freak, but at least his party of one is entertaining. I try for something non-committal. "And just ditch James?" *OhmygodOhmygod Ilikehim helikesme.*

Dean shrugs. "He's got a bus pass. Look, are you into me yet?"

I take a second to consider my options. Play innocent. That would be the pre-swim party Gretchen. Or, I could play this my (new) way. Get some balls, as James/Dean like to say.

He's watching, waiting, so I purr, "Yeah, I'm into you.

What do you want to do about it?"

I get the reaction I want: He's stunned. But only for a second. "Whoa — really? You serious? You'll go out with me?"

I flutter my eyelashes. I never knew I could be such a tease!

"Gretchen, I'm kind of blown away."

He's so cute. My name sounds so good when he says it. My name is a supermodel strutting down the runway of his tongue! *Gretchen! Gretchen!* "Gretchen?" James pokes his head through the window. His breath smells like onion chips. "You got any change? I'm short three bucks."

What Do I Say?

After fishing three dollars out of my pocket for James, I turn to Dean and say, "You want to take me for coffee?"

Why haven't I done this before — flirting with guys is the best thing! I feel like a lion tamer who's just made her cat jump through fire.

He's having trouble forming words, but when he does they're priceless: "Uh, yeah. Now?"

I slap his arm. "We can't leave James. He's your cousin."

"No, he's not," Dean says.

I suggest Wednesday. That gives me three days to prepare and him three days to sweat. I roll my head against the back of the seat, grinning at him.

He's finally catching up . . . and drooling.

"I'll pick you up from school."

James is walking toward us, a bag of Doritos in his hand — do guys never get sick of eating?

"Gretchen. Wednesday?" Dean puts his hand on my leg. HAND ON MY LEG.

I almost lose it.

James throws himself into the back seat and Lucy shudders to life.

I Have a DATE with

Basically an adult

A guy (duh)

A guy I like!

A guy who has his own car and a job

Who isn't in school

and likes to talk about things other than school

Who's my friend

Who likes me because I'm funny

and shares my devotion to grilled cheese sandwiches.

Why did I say Wednesday — it's so far away!

Forewoman Duties

The Spring Fair is fast approaching, according to Ashlyn, whose blood pressure must be through the roof. Even though they mostly look to me now, she marches around the kitchen, barking orders about how, what and why to bake. They all look at me behind her back, but I can only do so much. She did pull my butt out of the gutter not that long ago.

Okay, maybe it wasn't that dramatic. I owe the girl. We organize an assembly line of brownie makers. I get to be foreman (forewoman?) and deal with soaking dried cherries. We practise our roles like a circus troupe before the first night.

Just then Luke walks in with a shoebox under his arm and a foul look on his face. He heads for Ashlyn so fast he might just bowl her over.

"What the hell is this?" he snarls.

She looks panicked and whispers something. "Well, I DON'T WANT IT!" he shouts. "Stop following me around like a stalker! We are not together anymore!"

He turns and marches out, and Ashlyn leans on the counter, clutching the shoebox.

Since I'm forewoman, I rush over and offer assistance.

She glances around and mumbles, "Please, Gretchen, I can't handle them staring."

Do I Know About Public Humiliation?

Ashlyn bends over the sink
in the girls' washroom and tries to wipe
the mascara from her cheeks.
She looks like a sad clown.
I feel bad for ever thinking
evil thoughts about her. This
isn't far off what I went through
with Nemiah, and I'm not immune
to the irony.

"He said he loved me two weeks ago,"
she sniffs. I hand her a wad
of paper towel. "He said it and we
messed around and he stopped calling me."
Sounds like the kind of thing a jerk
would do, I just didn't think Luke
was one. I shake my mistaken head.
"He's a loser then. Forget him."
"I can't!" she cries. "I love him!
We were going to the Formal together!"

She doesn't explain what's in the shoebox,
and this doesn't seem
like a good time for me to ask. But then,
a stalker's a stalker.

"Ashlyn, you have to get over him.
Plus, there are people in there
who want to know if their brownie
batter is good enough." I point
out the door. I go on about boys being
the devil's spawn, and I don't think
she believes me (I don't), but she washes
her face and forces
a smile as we walk into the hall.
"Can I call you later, just to talk?"

I'm not sure I want to be Ashlyn's
sob sister, but part of me
remembers what it was like
to have that kind of girlfriend,
so I don't say no.

Phone Encounter

I have Dean's cell number taped to the inside of my desk at
home (and on speed dial, and in my journal, and burned
into my memory forever), and because I'm a loser and
obsessed and probably going to regret it, I call him before
I go to bed, just to say hi. He answers after five rings. Each
ring is a stone against my heart: he has call display. Does
he not want to talk to me?

"Hey, beautiful," he says finally, and I melt.

"Hi! Just wanted to say goodnight — you busy?" My own voice is pathetic in my ears.

He pauses. "Nah, just got home from work. You busy?"

I tell him I'm in bed (truth), just reading (lie).

"In bed, eh? Just had to mention that, didn't you?"

My face feels red hot. Thank god he can't see me.

"You're blushing!" he crows. How can he know? I thrash around to look out the window, my heart pounding. He cracks up. "I'm joking. It was a guess — but I was right!"

I don't fall asleep for two hours.

Social Chemistry

At our table in the library, I try to focus on the chemistry mumbo-jumbo before me. I finally get to the end of the chapter (James is taking a hands-off approach and making me actually do the work myself. Turd.) and he nods his approval, holding up a page he's been scratching notes on as I worked.

"So, I've been thinking about how social structures can be like chemical structures. There's this concept that society is a social molecule and social interactions are like molecular interactions."

He hands me the page. "Check it out."

Geekiness

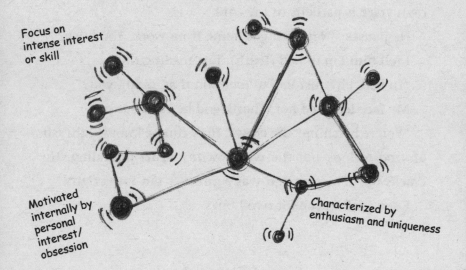

Focus on intense interest or skill

Motivated internally by personal interest/ obsession

Characterized by enthusiasm and uniqueness

Coolness

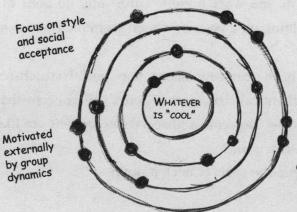

Focus on style and social acceptance

WHATEVER IS "COOL"

Motivated externally by group dynamics

Concerned with fitting in and avoiding uniqueness

It's strangely beautiful and oddly . . . poetic. How can it all fit so neatly into these categories?

"So you are . . . one of the geeks?" I point to the molecular structure.

"Well, this might be chemistry geeks, all connected by one obsession or skill. You would have your own poetry geek–shaped molecule."

"Enough with the —"

James interrupts me with a roll of his eyes. "Yes, you are, Gretchen. You're in the food club and you are poetry obsessed. Those are, in fact, two areas of geekiness for my one."

I stare down at the paper. "Fine. Say I am. Why are the other people circling an empty space? Shouldn't there be something in there — like a nucleus?"

He looks impressed. "Actually, the point is that the cool people are bonded by their idea of whatever is cool. It could be anything, so each cool group is different. The thing is that the individuality of those people can't be expressed if it doesn't conform to whatever is 'cool'." Again, the air quotes.

"So . . . ?"

He taps the page. "So maybe there are geeks trapped inside the bodies of jocks and hot girls all over this school, and no one has been able to get them out."

"Psst."

We both jump at the sound over James's shoulder. Next,

a wad of paper bounces off his binder and rolls between us. I turn to see two of the guys who de-t-shirted James walking out of the library, heads down as if nothing happened.

James has opened the paper and flattened it in front of him. It's blank, but from the look on his pale face, this isn't the first time.

Haiku for Sushi

Surprise! wrapped in rice
a good day dipped in soy sauce
Warning! Wasabi!

My New Best Friend

Guess who?

We
thankfully
have almost no classes
together, but Ashlyn
has managed to find me
three times today and offered me
her muffin, to loan me her coat,
to have me over for dinner,
to show me her family's
new litter of beagle puppies.

I
don't mind,
considering what happened.
I guess it's expected,
and I won't turn down
the attention. But it feels
a little weird to be followed
so closely by someone
so new. I agree to the muffin
but nothing else.

Familial Interlude

I've been so wrapped up in my burgeoning social life that I haven't been around the house much. I haven't had to watch any of Layla's brain-numbing dances or listen to my parents' reminders about good grades and medical school-related extracurriculars. Honestly, I've been keeping to myself a lot since the slam. It's self-preservation that results in a lot of eating of cereal in my room.

But maybe Mum and Dad sense this with their offspring-happiness-radars, because tonight we are having Family Pasta Night. Family make-noodles-from-scratch-each-other's-eyeballs-out night.

I'm told this when I get home from school. Only an hour to mentally prepare for the onslaught.

Pasta Wranglers

Layla and I have been making pasta for a few years now, so even though I don't want to be here at all, at least I know what I'm doing. She and I are on roll 'n' crank duty. We roll and crank the pasta dough through the machine until it comes out in long, playdough ribbons, which we lay out and then put in boiling water. I can tell the fun of doing all this is wearing thin with her too. We both used to love it, fought over who did what.

Now I have to be dragged in and I wager next year she will too. Mum's on sauce duty, but she eyes us as we roll and crank. "Isn't this nice, girls? We don't do this enough these days." I know she sees what's happening. Her little girls are growing out of pasta wrangling — what on earth can she do?

"There's more dough? I thought we were done!" Layla wails.

"Only another few sheets." Mum leaves the sauce to help. I take over stirring, thankful for the switch-up. Layla gives me a look that says, "You cow, how could you leave me here?" Mum sees it, square on. Like the look was meant for her.

Food Club Blues

I am over being forewoman.
So, so over it. Since I'm Ashlyn's
new saviour, she asked me
to take on extra duties, and these
include shepherding those
with the littlest brains so they
don't burn or drop things,
and then cleaning up
after they do a shoddy job
cleaning up the kitchen.
If I have to chip off any more
pasta dough dried like glue
on the counters
when I could be doing anything else
I'll freak.

Warning

Mr. Marchand is once again the bearer of bad news; my progress report will show a pitiful chemistry grade, much too low for The Board's standards. Not a fail, thanks to James, but still: undoctorly.

But there are other far more pressing matters on the horizon, and I push everything else out of my mind . . .

Countdown

Today is the day.
Now is the time:
3:30 P.M., and I'm pretending
to read my social studies homework,
waiting for the clock
to get to 4:00 P.M.,
so I can walk outside
and look like I almost
wasn't going to make it.

Flawless casual-looking makeup: check.
Slightly messy but perfect hair: check.
Jeans that give good butt: check.
Lucky bra: check. (It's not really lucky,
but after this it will be!)
Heart in throat: check.
Maybe I should check my pulse —
Be cool. I search for the bitchin' attitude
I had in the car the day I asked him out.
Well, asked him to ask me out.

Breathe in.
Okay, go.

8

IT'S A DATE

Dean Pulls Up

looking so . . . touchable in a blue-collared shirt, with a bouquet of daisies lying on the passenger seat. I'm in trouble.

He gets out and opens the door for me, gives me a hug and the flowers. "I know we're just going for coffee, but I wanted to get you something."

He shifts the car with finesse and we drive away from the school, away from my boring life as a nobody in grade eleven, and toward —

We Get Married in the Coffee Shop

My dress is made of white linen napkins
stitched together, and the manager
of the place marries us, with the baristas
as witnesses. We have blueberry coffee
cake and chai tea at the reception.

Reality: We Get Chatting in the Coffee Shop

We talk about music and Japanese food, what we want to be, what we don't want to be.

He asks if I've told The Board about our date.

"It's not really their business," I say. I don't say I haven't even told them about him at all.

"Won't they approve?" he teases.

"Who cares if they don't? I want something just for myself," I say, leaning in enough to make him catch his breath.

He can't stop looking at me and I have this squishy feeling in my stomach. My chai tea and blueberry coffee cake are only half-drunk/eaten because we've been talking so much.

By 5:46 I realize we could go on like this all night.

"You need to go?" he asks.

"No, I'll just make a call," I say, and get up, pulling out my first generation phone.

"Whoa, that's old school!" he says and grabs for it.

"Yes, I know, it's been passed down through the family for hundreds of years."

He laughs, examining the phone like it's actually an antique.

"I thought everyone was born with one of *these* nowadays." He holds out his shiny version.

I take it from him and tease, "Who says *nowadays* nowadays?"

He pokes me in the stomach and I squeal.

A few old people look up from their coffees and frown.

Ringtone Love

Before he drops me off at the end of my driveway,
he leans over like he's going to kiss me,
instead shows me his phone.
"Guess what you are?" he says.

"Um, a great catch?"
"For sure," he laughs. "But I mean
your ringtone. James is the Star Wars theme.
My dad is Darth Vader."

"Really?"
He shrugs. "I was kind of pissed at him
when I programmed it, but now it fits.
He gets a kick out of it."

He looks at me with the cutest, waiting-est
look on his face.
"Um, an ewok?" I ask,
inside thinking, *please be Princess Amidala, please
be Princess Amidala.*

He finds my name in his phone
and Natalie Portman's voice makes me smile.

The Wrong Girl

I come through the door a respectable thirteen minutes before the nine o'clock deadline and they are all sitting on the couch watching *The Muppet Show*. Really. For a second I wonder if I've stepped into a time warp.

"How was it?" Layla asks suspiciously, as if she knows it was not a visit to Ashlyn's house, which is my cover.

"Fine. We went over Spring Fair stuff. Her dog just had a litter of puppies. We played with them." I lean against the back of the couch. "Why are you watching this?"

"Your sister's choice. It brings us back to our first days in Canada," my dad says. "I learned English from shows like this."

It's oddly disturbing to see them all together on the couch, doing something so familial without me. Not that I wanted to be here at all. "Well, I'm going to do my homework. Goodnight." I turn to go.

"We're due a progress report soon, aren't we?" my mum says.

I shrug. "I guess."

"And we're really pleased to hear about the initiative you're showing with the Food Club. Good leadership skills."

I know where she's going with this. *These are all traits of a good doctor. We couldn't be happier that you are cramming yourself into the box we picked out for you!*

"Yeah, well . . ." I keep inching backwards, hoping they'll get distracted by Miss Piggy.

"By the way," Dad says. "My friend Harold — you remember him? — he says he'd be happy to have you visit him when he's working in the hospital so you can ask some questions and learn a little about what he does. Being an anaesthetist is very lucrative."

"Okay," I say. "I'm going to go now."

"That's very nice of him," Mum says. "Isn't it, Gretchen?"

"Yes, it's very nice of him. I'm tired, so . . ."

Finally something funny happens on the TV and Layla howls. I don't wait around to finish my sentence.

Reliving Heaven

It was so dreamy, so amazing, so adjective adjective adjective!

There aren't words in the English language, or any other, to describe the way he leaned in, so slowly, the shudder of Lucy a background hum. The way his clothes smelled, the coffee on his breath, his lips, so close.

I think I blacked out from that kiss — but maybe not — I remember the feel of our mouths together, the warm wet (way better than behind the portables). I felt shivery and fevery, goose pimply. He smiled into my neck as we hugged.

I could feel it, and I wanted to drive away with him. It was like we could have lived off that feeling for the rest of our lives.

Small Miracle

At 9:37, seven minutes
after incoming calls
are disallowed (except Nemiah's
back in the age of that friendship),
there's a knock on my door,
and I look up from my social studies text
to see Layla holding the phone out.
It's Ashlyn.
Bless Ashlyn and all her weirdness
for her good timing.
She's calling to whine about Luke,
but also to blab about
the Spring Fair. I let her
talk while I finish the last two
comprehension questions.
I don't want to be rude — after all
she called just in time
to make my cover story appear true.
In the end, I agree to help all day
at the baking table so she won't
lose her mind without me.
Friends help each other, right?

Spring Fair Dress Rehearsal
(cue dramatic music)

It has arrived faster than I expected, with all the excitement of a medieval execution. Everyone is thrilled to bake enough brownies to kill an army and then hawk them behind a table like a seller at ye olde carnival. And, amazingly, the fair's not for another ten days. There's still lots of procrastination time, but we are all in the Foods room to see how efficient we can be. I wonder if this is like the pep talk the swim team gets.

Coach Ashlyn paces and throws out words like stamina, perseverance and silicone oven mitts. She pounds her fist into her hand and for once, everyone is listening instead of looking to me. I'm a little proud of her, actually.

We organize ingredients, roll up our sleeves and get to work. Garth/Thor is on chocolate chip duty and I wrangle the little-brains so they don't mistake baking powder for flour. It all goes like clockwork.

Ashlyn is so happy she wears a perma-smile. "It's going to be so amazing, don't you think, Gretchen?" I agree as I help avert an egg-cracking disaster.

"Hey," she says, "you want to come to my place tomorrow night? I'd love to go through some other recipes I found online. And you've got to see the puppies — they're the cutest things ever!" I glance around, hating to let her down in so public a place.

"Maybe," I say, and then make a huge mistake. "I might be doing something with my boyfriend."

Echoes in the Foods Room

"Boyfriend?"
Garth/Thor stands behind us, his hands full
of melting chocolate chips. "Gretchen
has a boyfriend?"
Ashlyn turns to me.
"You have a boyfriend? Oh my god!
Is it someone I know?"
I try to back away, but a little-brain says,
"It's James Tarden in grade twelve!"
There are giggles. Snickers. All baking ceases.
"Some people saw you two leaving school
a bunch of times," says the little-brain.
"Is he the guy with the t-shirts that tell
everyone they're so much stupider
than him?" someone calls.
"Oh my god, are you two going out?"
I am speechless for a moment, and then
I am overwhelmed with fury.
"You freaks!" I spit. "James is a really nice guy."
"You *are* going out with him!" people shout.
"No, I'm not!" I yell. "It's someone else!"
But by then the damage is done.

The Bus Stop

He stands in a jagged line of bus-waiters, brown t-shirt proclaiming the formula for some chemical I'd rather not think about. It shouldn't bother me — he knows who he is and I respect that — but after the last hour of fending off questions about our supposed romantic entanglement, it would be better if his t-shirt was plain.

He looks around as if he's searching for someone but his face opens into a smile when he sees me. "Hey, Gretchen. Ready for bowling insanity tonight? I'm terrible, but I'm told I'm entertaining to watch."

I turn my back on the people staring at us. Apparently news travels fast from the Foods room.

He keeps looking over his shoulder.

"What's going on?" I ask. "You're acting kind of twitchy."

He leans in, still looking around. "Pulled a prank on the lacrosse team. Tell no one."

I mouth the word "what" and make it a question with my raised eyebrows.

The bus turns the corner and the waiters scramble to be first in line for the empty seats. James steps back and I follow.

"These guys have been accosting me for months. I couldn't handle it anymore." He looks down at his runners, one corner of his mouth pulling up. "Ammonium sulphide, kids."

"Oh, god — did you poison them?"

He rolls his eyes as the bus pulls to a stop. "No — it's a stink bomb, Gretchen. Don't you remember anything from our lessons?" He steps into line and waves. "See you tonight."

The Truth Hurts

Grades in hand, I walk into the living room, unable to delay any longer. I know it's better they hear it from me.

I shove the paper at them and hold my breath as they scan it. Force myself to breathe.

They're quick to spot the incongruity.

"What happened here?" Dad says, pointing. "You didn't tell us your chemistry grade was so weak."

"I got a tutor. And I didn't fail, so that's good."

"What kind of tutor was it? This is a very low mark." Mum shakes her head. "Why didn't you tell us about this? We could have found you someone professional, someone —"

"I didn't want that. God, I didn't want a tutor in the first place. I hate chemistry and it's a miracle I passed."

"Well, you'll need to pull up this grade if you want to get into pre-med. We can find you someone. Margaret next door knows a university student who —"

"You're not listening." I pull the paper from their hands. "I. Hate. Chemistry. I'm going to drop it as soon as I can so I can focus on stuff I really care about . . ." Deep breath. "And I don't want to be a doctor."

They stare, of course. "But you've always said . . ."

"I haven't wanted to be a doctor for about a decade. It was you who wanted me to be one." I hold out my grades again. "Look: A+ in English. I want to be a writer. That's what I love."

"When did you decide this?" Dad says. "It doesn't sound like you."

"Actually it sounds exactly like me," I say.

My mum is looking uneasily at the floor. "You did mention it, Gretchen, but you know it's not a realistic career choice. How would you support yourself on writing?"

I scrunch up the paper and watch them cringe. "God, no one understands me but my friends."

"And who are these friends? Is it Ashlyn?"

"It's James and Dean, the guys I've hung out with for weeks. The guys who were there after Nemiah —" I stop. "Anyway, they understand."

Mum picks the crumbled paper off the floor. "You haven't told us about these boys. What do you do with them? Who are they?"

God, they didn't give Layla this much third degree about Wes. "What does it matter? We hang out. They're great guys." Then I make a mistake. "We're going out tonight."

"No, you're not," Dad says. "We need to talk about this. You can't expect us to let you go out after this conversation, without meeting these boys, not knowing where you're going."

"I'm sixteen, Dad. We're going bowling. In public. End of

story." I start to walk away, anger filling my stride.

"You are not leaving this house, Gretchen," Mum says behind me. "We'll finish this over dinner."

"No, we won't," I say without turning. "I'm not hungry."

Forget This

I call Dean from my room. Since I'm already going down, might as well go all the way. I'll set my good-girl ways adrift for tonight. The tide's brought in another version of me.

I tell him to wait on the street — I can get to the back door without going past the kitchen.

Low voices float, knives and forks scrape plates. I take a step — and put my toe into mashed potatoes. Someone's left a plate of food in front of my door.

My phone vibrates in my pocket and makes me jump. It's Dean. His name glows, teasing me.

I push the plate out of the way, smear food into the carpet, sneak down the hall,

step out of my life.

9

BOWLING FAIL

The Way There

"James has his own ride," he says even before I ask.
"Does he not want to drive with us?" I say, buckling up.
Dean leans over and kisses my cheek,
turns me into a puddle on the floor.
"He got to borrow his mum's car, which never happens.
He's pretty stoked." He puts a hand on my leg.
My skin tingles. I squeeze his long, strong fingers.

It feels so good to be a girlfriend, riding alone
with Dean. James's absence is actually a relief.
We laugh and ride, holding hands,
feeling what it feels like to be a couple, just us.
I find myself wishing we weren't
going bowling with James and a ton of other people.

We pass Mosquito Creek Park and I think about us

pulling in there, taking off layers of clothes.

My skin tingles.

Suddenly Dean's turning left, reading my mind,

which is racing.

Detour

I don't even get my seat belt off and he's kissing me, pulling me toward him, and I have to laugh and unclip the belt, and we kiss again. His tongue is warm and tastes like toothpaste, and I never knew that could be sexy. He runs his hand under my shirt and over my skin, not going for the bra clips, which makes me wish he would.

"You're so beautiful," he whispers. And I want to run away forever with him, just leave this place and be together, alone.

I kiss him hard and reach under his shirt — his skin is so soft and it makes me want to feel the rest of him.

But then his phone sings the Star Wars theme.

"Oh, god," Dean groans. "He can wait."

James goes to voicemail and Dean pulls me from my seat, into his lap. My leg is pinned against the door but I don't care — his hands are under my waistband, feeling my butt, his warm hands, his minty breath on my —

The Empire strikes back. We both groan, our mouths still together.

Thirty seconds later, the Jedi returns. He must be pissed.

Dean adjusts himself as I pull my shirt back down and grab his phone.

"Hey, James," I say in a cheery voice. "We're just leaving my place. Sorry we're late."

"Yeah," he says, in a galaxy far, far away. "Whatever, face-munchers."

Bowling

I'm not one for the nostalgic fifties bowling thing, but it is amazing how many people like it. We descend into the weird time-warped, neon-lit basement and search for James in the bowling-shoed, shirt-collared crowd — this is teen night; everyone plays for five bucks.

We spot James, wearing his *Geeks Rule the World* shirt, by the jukebox. He flips through the song book and we sneak up behind him, ready to pounce. That's when I notice the guys by the shoe bar (that's what I call it) staring at us.

No — they're staring at James.

They're S&E — I recognize a few from the lacrosse team. Their faces are stone.

I say a loud *hi* to James — and then remember what he told me at the bus stop. I touch his shoulder. "James, did you —"

"You guys want to hear some Elvis?" he interrupts me.

"Of course we don't," Dean laughs. "Play something from this century."

James won't look at me.

I'm not sure how to broach the subject because every-one's acting so weird. The lacrosse guys move to the other end of the bowling alley and we wait in awkward silence for our lane to open up.

Gutter Ball

The bowling doesn't go well. James is quiet and I'm bowl-ing like a granny — literally.

Dean makes fun of my technique and I have to punch him in the stomach — and end up feeling his abs. So firm.

He squeezes my waist. James goes for a Coke.

"He seems kind of zoned out," Dean says. "Maybe we should hang out somewhere else." I put my head on his shoulder.

"I hate high school," I mutter. "People suck."

Just then, speak of the devil, in saunters the swim team — really, the WHOLE swim team. Shay's at the helm and Nemiah's in the middle, literally mediocre, and they all do a lap of the place before settling at the snack tables with their tiny skirts and perky ponytails. The swim guys lean on their ripped forearms and try not to topple over from the weight of their massive shoulders.

"See that?" I point to Nemiah in her solid pink velour tracksuit. "That's the opposite of class."

She's become a stick of bubble gum. How apt.

Triangle

We play another game
and James bowls gutters every time,
which makes him even more pissed off.
He seems to be taking offense to me and Dean
sharing the same chair.
"You know there are empty seats right here,"
he says. "There's no need to conserve."
"She's my lap-warmer," Dean says,
and James looks away.
I've never seen him like this
and I start to think it's my fault — our fault —
for being so together in from of him
when something happens that
makes it all seem like
nothing.

Catalyst

It only takes one look —
James walking to the washroom
past a posse of reclining lacrosse guys,
glancing over at them
for a nanosecond —
I see it because I'm so on edge
I can't help watching him —
and just one guy

gives a flick of the hand,
some signal to strike,
and they all launch as one hulking mass
onto James's back.

The Next Thing I Know

they are on the floor,
a storm of flailing limbs, and then
the swim team is hurtling into the fray,
their fists like maces. They grab indiscriminately —
a fight's a fight.
Dean is gone from beside me,
     swallowed by the brawl.
I realize I am screaming
     like everyone else.
The alley manager,
     a brawny guy
          in head-to-toe denim,
wades into the fight
and fishes James out. Dean
     is still somewhere inside.
          Denim Man bellows one
          long roar, and the fighters
cease like a pack of dogs
     sprayed with a hose.
I rush up to James

and look past him
as Dean extricates himself
from a swim boy's clutches.
"Who started this?" Denim Man asks.
"WHO STARTED THIS?!"
Five fingers point to James.
Dean starts to protest
but Denim Man yells,
"Get out now — all of you
          or I'll call the cops."

Dean Grabs James

and I follow them outside,
across the street and up the road
to James's car.
He doesn't get in, just stands
on the frosty cement
and gulps frozen air.

His left eye is swelling up.

I pace to try and stop my body
trembling. My fingertips
are ice cold.

Attempt

Dean tries to touch James's shoulder,
       tries to say calming things
in a low voice,
but James is wound tight, can't hear him,
shoves his hand away.
"I can't believe," he says.
"I can't believe those freaking —"
"How come they can —"
He shakes his head.

"Let's go," Dean says.
"My place. We'll get cleaned up."

James looks at him, then at me.
"No," he says. "I need to drive.
This is my thing. I need to think.
You guys go ahead."

"You shouldn't go alone," I say
but it feels flimsy —
I'm with Dean and it's obvious
James doesn't want to be reminded of that.

"You can't help," he says
as I open my mouth to protest again.

We watch him get into the car and drive away.
It feels like the wrong choice, but
we also have no choice — he doesn't want us.
What can we do? I think. *What can we do?*

"We can go home," Dean says beside me,
taking my hand, answering the question
I didn't think I'd said out loud.

We Drive

I'm not ready to go home yet, and anyway,
I'm worried about James, alone in his car.
Dean murmurs to me like someone
calming a horse. My stomach flutters
at the low sound.
"I told my parents about wanting to be a writer,"
I say quietly.
"Right on. I'm proud of you," he says in
such a gentle way I don't want to say
anything else, to ruin it with how badly
the conversation went.
We drive to the end of a cul-de-sac with big,
expensive houses. A playground emerges on the right.
"Come on the slide with me." Dean says,
and it seems like the best idea in the world.
My brain goes blank as I close the cold door, my skin

tingly, warmed from the car.
It's the chaos, the shock of everything
that makes him so irresistible, makes me
follow him
anywhere.

Slide

The playground
has never been a more fascinating place,
full of kid things that are transformed
in the dark,
places to hide and kiss
and touch.
Frost covers everything like velvet.
We brush it away
with our sleeved hands
he lays his jacket down,
we sit at the top of the slide
and feel each other's skin.

Dean's breath is hot
on my mouth,
his fingers travelling
under my bra strap,
burning my skin,
making my heart crash in my chest.

A dog barks from across the street,
startles us, giggling, down the slide.
The stars are so still and white
from my position
in Dean's lap.
We laugh
as a distant siren makes the dog
howl.

Details Aside

We get pretty close to something
in that park,
but I'm not going to go there
here.
Let's just say
!!

Vibrations

Once we're back in the car, my phone tells me someone's
left a message. My gut twists: my parents must be freaking.
Until this moment I've forced myself to forget the shackles,
possible electric chair awaiting me.

We sit in Lucy, talking and kissing with the heat blasted.
My hormones have started to drain out of invisible holes
in my skin.

I just feel tired and stupid.

Dean's phone rings. I jump out of my seat, wondering how my parents got a hold of his number.

It's not them. Someone's yelling on the other end. Dean holds the phone from his ear, trying to decipher the voice.

"He what?" he finally says.

There's a pause on the line and then I hear the reply from across the car.

10

IT'S NOT GOOD

The Drive

is full of nothing-noise: the shudder of Lucy's old-car body, the whine of her tired engine, the rumble of other cars on the street. Dean pops his jaw over and over.

I try to ask questions and he won't stop talking, the words jumble up in his mouth.

He tells me what he knows: James was driving his mum's car on the highway and there was a collision, we don't know with what yet. The car is totalled.

He's in the ICU, unconscious and unstable and who knows what else. His mother's been there since they brought him in. She's the one who called Dean.

And, oh god, it's his fault, his stupid fault, Dean says, then clamps his mouth shut. Our make-out session at the park seems idiotic now. I can't clear my throat.

Dean signals to turn into the parking lot but turns on the windshield wipers by accident.

What Does Someone in the ICU Look Like?

I realize I've never been
in a hospital like this before.

Once I went to see my aunt,
dying of cancer, but I was ten

and we didn't stay long.
Will he be all wrapped up,

with wires and IVs everywhere?
Will there be blood?

My heart rams into my ribs
and I grip Dean's hand

which is sweaty and cold.

It's Bad

My first look at him,
I know.
Unstable
is scarier than it sounds.

Face

James's unconscious face is swollen huge
on one side, bandaged and gruesome.
Ugly bruises deform him into a troll.
He isn't even breathing on his own —
a machine does it for him,
through a tube down his throat.
It all looks fake.

How could this have happened?
Two hours ago he was fine.

His mother is a small woman
with dark brown hair
and a face hidden in the green
hospital sheet on her son's
bed. She looks up with puffy
red eyes and a small, quivering
mouth.

Haiku: Life Draining

out through snaking tubes
what are they putting back in?
Put his LIFE back in!

Constance

is a tall, thin woman with frizzy blond hair
in old-fashioned clips. She stands to shake our hands.
She holds a clipboard, a pen, the answers
to all our questions.
She is the social worker.
The sympathetic ear assigned to James's family
because his injuries are so traumatic
they don't want us to keel over from shock
or get violent. She is a walking, talking
pacifier.
Dean ignores her.

He Walks

straight-faced to the bed,
amid the beeping of machines
the hard breathing
of James's mother,
the screaming
in my head.

This is
so unnatural, unfair, unbelievable,
un-everything.
My hands make fists.
Bad dream bad dream bad dream.
Wake up.
Wake up, James.

The Situation

is dire, we learn from Dr. Ziola, a warm-eyed,
pretty doctor who seems out of place in this terrible world.
James has serious head trauma. There is
some internal bleeding,
they don't know how much yet.
They are trying to get his hemoglobin up
so he can make it through surgery.
He can make it. Dean latches onto this idea,
turns the *can* into a *will*. The doctor
tries to offer reality, but Dean isn't listening.

I look around
at all the life-saving equipment,
the things that exist for the purpose
of helping people not die.

Five Minutes Later

A nurse comes in to take some readings.
We all stare at her, at the machines telling her things
we want to know, even if we can't understand them.
Constance speaks to us in low tones,
comforting, like a hostage negotiator.
I want to smack her and hug her at the same time.

James's mum paces, holds her head in her hands,
like a grieving parent in a movie.

The nurse looks at the machines,
does something to the IV bag.
She leaves, rustling in her green scrubs.

I put a hand on Dean's. I know what he's thinking,
and I tell him it's not his fault. Not our fault. For letting
James leave the bowling alley, for not doing something
different. But I know my words aren't getting through.
He's torturing himself already:

I, I, I could have stopped this.

I want to echo: no, no, no, you couldn't

but could we have?

Beep-Beep

A machine drones. Little lights blink.
The nurse returns.
I come back from the grey place where I was drifting.
We are in Sickland. James is not dead.
His *Geeks Rule the World* t-shirt is gone
who knows where,
ripped off in efforts to discover his injuries,
but suddenly it means so much more.
It means everything.

The beeping beeps.
The machines hold James's life, and they are only machines.

1:13 A.M.

I finally check my messages.
There are five.
Halfway through
the third one,
as my mum's voice falters,
my eyes fill up.
I make myself listen
to them all.
They have called everyone they know,
everyone in the school,
even Ms Long.

I can't
I can't call when everything's uncertain
everyone's rushing,
questioning, waiting.
But the empty-belly feeling
of not calling them
eats me until I am a shell,
full of nothing.

Just when I thought
it was so great to not listen for once,
I replay
the messages,
listen
to hear how much they want me home.

Good Enough

Dr. Ziola tells us they have to take James for surgery.
He's as stable as he's going to get
and they can't wait any longer.

This isn't reassuring.

Dean wants to know that he's going to make it.
He prods and prods to get this answer
and finally

Constance has to take him out into the hall.
I can hear him hyperventilating.
I stay for James's mother,
who looks like her life is being taken
away on that hospital bed.
There is nothing I can do that is of use.
I back up to the door, equidistant
between the grieving mother and cousin,
and act as a doorstop.

Dean Paces

in the hall: down, turn,
back again, down.
His face is like
stretched canvas
over sharp bones.
He doesn't see anything —
not me, not the passing
nurses or doctors,
not the old man on a gurney
watching him with sad eyes.
Then they wheel James out,
carefully, quickly, no more
explanation,
ignoring Dean's frantic questions,
and even after they're gone,

he asks more,

like a lost, demented parrot.

Then Dean Takes Off

And I am chasing him down the hall,

into the stairwell,

down two flights, three flights,

knees buckling, going so fast.

I yell for him to slow down. He screams wordlessly.

We run down, down — how much down is there?

We run into the basement

and I remember from TV and movies

this is where the morgue must be.

I catch up to Dean,

or he slows down for me,

and we stop, breathing hard, our knees

jittery. He doesn't push

the door open. He knows

what's in there.

This is the underworld.

He Folds

into a ball on the shiny
stairwell floor.
No crying, just silence, his eyes
staring empty, chin on knees. I sit beside him,
shoulder touching his.
He whispers,
"He has to be okay.
This is crazy, right?
He can't — no, he can't.
It's okay."
He doesn't know I'm here.
I grope for something to say
that will make it okay, but nothing will.
I can't even give him
a piece of hope —
I can't give myself that.

Surfacing

After a while the silence is too strong.

"I'm going up," I say, touching his cold hand. "I want to
know what's happening. They might have an update from
the surgery."

Dean looks at me slowly. He is past words.

If I push him over, he'll shatter.

But I can't stay down here, not breathing.

I backtrack up the stairwell, my hands numb, my mind
blinking like a traffic light in a power outage.

How Many Hours

have gone by since I got back?
One? Five? A hundred?
I sit in the ICU waiting room
with a family from Bolivia
waiting to find out about their grandfather.
James's mother is phoning relatives from the hall —
I focus on the wallpaper so as not to hear
her repeated sobs.

I pull out
my cellphone and dial home,
hang up, then repeat this three times.

Dawn

Not the real one —
a metaphorical one.
The one where I realize,
as I'm about to press call,
that maybe they won't understand.
Maybe they will yell and scream
and not be sad for me,
for James, for this night
of terrible things.

I'm sorry for sneaking out,
I'm sorry for stepping in the mashed potatoes
and smearing them into the carpet,
I'm sorry for leaving James
when he obviously needed me,
I'm sorry for not calling them
when they most want me to.

And

I think
of paging Constance
to tell her my skin
can't get warm —
could that be
a health concern
or just a symptom
of the night's events —
when Dr. Ziola walks in.
Her forehead
is wrinkled with concern.
She asks for James's mother.
She is found.
The last thing I wonder
before the doctor gives us the news
is if she has concern lines
like the rest of us have
laugh-lines.

doubles over, punched in the gut.
Her face is pulled tight.
I am frozen to the spot
and she reaches out,
clenches me. Her shirt,
her skin, smell like
cinnamon.
My face is buried in it.

Finally she looks up,
touches my wet face,
says words
only she can hear.

There Are No Words

Haiku: Spring Morning

Lukewarm sun hovers
on frosted tulips in the
hospital courtyard

Haiku: Spring Morning

Someone leaves a worn
blue teddy bear on James's
silent, still machines.

Haiku: Spring Morning

Sky bright white outside —
muddy black inside my chest.
Clouds cover over.

GONE

He Is Gone

He is gone he
is gone he
is gone
he is
gone he
is gone he
is gone he is
gone
he is gone he is gone
he is
gone
he is gone
he is
is
is
gone

Gone Is a Strange Word

if you look at it,
say it,
write it
long enough,
it starts
to change shape,
and sound,
and idea.
To detach
from its meaning.
What is
gone?

gone is being *not*

The Next Few Hours

are shifting grey, a sandstorm,
a handful of dust in the eyes.
Dean drives me to his place in silence.
I don't have the strength
or guts
to check my phone for new messages.
I know they'll think
I'm dead or kidnapped.
I'm too exhausted,
too consumed by the grey
to care.
We fall into Dean's bed,
cold, smooth, boy-blue sheets,
still in our coats,
and crash.

I Wake

to shifting light through curtains. The clock says 3:17 P.M.
We've slept for hours — through the whole day. Dean is
motionless, slow-breathing beside me. He looks so peaceful, so young. His cheek is pink and pillow-creased. I want
to touch the lines, but don't want to wake him.

I've pushed all thoughts from my mind, and this in-
between place is nice. It's calm, it doesn't hurt. I know when
he wakes up, the spell, the grey sand we're floating in, will

dissolve. We'll have to talk about what happened. Reality
will flood everything. I push these thoughts from my brain
for one last moment. Get up to find some breakfast.

He Finds Me

in the kitchen, munching dry cereal
out of the box.
"You want a shower?" he asks,
rubbing his eyes.
I consider this, my first shower
at a guy's house. A boyfriend's house.

He doesn't ask to join me,
but he does give me
a big, long kiss in the doorway
that makes me desperate
and sad and want to be close
to him forever. I fight
to stay in the grey place
a little longer.

"I'm out of milk," he says,
surveying the kitchen.
I squeeze his hand.
He smiles, slowly, as if it's
not just like breathing, to smile.

The Elephant in the Room

Dean won't talk about it. I sit with him on the couch, try to reach him with my hands and my voice and finally tears. He won't talk about it.

As I cry, last night comes clear, the grey cloud evaporating around me, making everything too bright and loud and sharp. The beep of machines, shouts of nurses as they wheeled James down the hall, James's mother, her eyes, her sobs like tearing fabric in my ear.

We have to call her. It feels like I'm underwater, weighed down by a thousand stones, but I still try to move.

Everything takes so much effort.

But Dean gets up to have a shower.

He hasn't left the grey place.

Part of Me

wants to go back there too,
to be with him
and forget all the terrible sounds
and flashing pictures.
But I can't.

I'm here,
we're still here, and James
isn't.

Attempt

I spend the next two hours tip-toeing around Dean. He's trying to pretend nothing happened. I'm not allowed to mention it, and if I look like I'm going to cry, he leaves the room. I cry alone.

I creep into his bedroom to find him reading a sci-fi magazine, a slight frown-line across his forehead.

"Hey," I whisper.

"Uhn," he answers. "You hungry?"

I shake my head, tell him we should call James's mother, make sure she's okay.

His face turns to stone.

"Come on, Dean —"

"No. Just stop."

I start to explain what I know is true, what he knows: James is gone, gone, gone. We're sad, sad, sad. My jaw aches from trying not to cry and for a second I think he's shifting to hug me —

But Instead

he grabs me by the shoulders, his arms shaking, growls, "Shut up, okay?" He throws me back on the bed. "Just leave me alone."

I scramble up, adrenaline pulsing in my muscles. I want to run, get out and keep going.

He looks guilty, rubs his face like a little boy.

150

He holds out his hand, pleading.

I so want to reach for him, but I can't, I can't.

I reach for my phone.

12

GOODBYE

Breakfast

Mum comes into my room
with a tray: orange juice,

toast and jam. A piece
of chocolate. She lays it

on the floor because she thinks
I'm sleeping.

Chocolate is not usually
a breakfast food, even

around here. But it's a new era.
None of us knows the rules yet.

Caution

That feeling
of carefully manoeuvring
around someone so you don't upset them —
watch what you say,
what you do,
what you don't say or do.

That's us. We all have light shields around us
to deflect incoming missiles.

Layla's afraid to look at me.
My mother talks to her hands, the wall,
my ear, like I'm someone
she's just met, doesn't know how to gage.
My dad thinks I'll run away again,
but he also wants to punish me —
I can see the battle on his face.

I wander aimlessly
trying to get away from the ache
between my shoulder blades.

We have a stalemate. Except it feels
like everyone loses.

Another Strange Word

Funeral.

Sunday.
James's mother calls, gives details,
tries not to break down
on the phone. I nod to her questions
as if she can see me.
Remember my voice to say goodbye.

Sunday.

Sometime Later

I wake up from a daydream
(daynightmare?)
at the kitchen table,
my Cheerios a soggy beige mush,
and realize I really don't know
how Dean is.
I haven't talked to Dean
— in two days?
Why haven't I thought of him?
Guilt rises in my throat
and I toss the Cheerio mush
down the sink. Grab
the phone.

No Answer

Hey, it's Gretchen. Sorry I've been out of it for a while. I
guess you have too. Just call me when you get this, okay?
I miss you.

My Parents Try

to get me cornered
and talk about my situation.

My mother stares at my chin

and murmurs words
of forgiveness followed by an if-clause
Dad gets frustrated,
        not knowing who I am
and leaves the meeting
early.

I don't know who I am,
        I want to say
but all they do is push words
at me
words that tell me who I should be:

You're always so responsible,
mature, honest, blah
        blah
blah

I don't have the energy
to speak, argue, breathe

"We'll drive you to the funeral,"
Mum says as she gets up.
This I didn't expect.

"Come with me," I say.

Haiku: Funeral

White fingertips clutch
glossy oak casket, while birds
sing life into spring

Haiku: Funeral

James's mother lost
in a wide sea of green grass.
Her black heels sink in.

Haiku: Funeral

Dean's not here. Dean is
nowhere. Dean has forgotten
himself, somewhere else.

Gathering

We get there early,
my parents and I.
I'll give it to them — they are sad
about James. They don't know him
but they wear black.
James's mother
hugs me, greets others,
shakes hands. Ms Long
appears, gives me a shoulder squeeze
and then heads for James's family.
It's a gathering for a dead boy, with carnations,
baby's breath, soft music.
But everything is colourless,
like I'm wearing
black-and-white glasses.
The ache between my shoulders
makes me reach for two Advil.
I swallow them dry,
but the ghost of them sticks
to the back of my throat.

Mourning

Funerals work on different time —
an hour taking a day, an afternoon
lasting a year, all the seasons
going by as you watch
in slow motion.

We wait for the far-flung family
to arrive — cousins and grandparents,
shaking hands, mopping faces,
each saying thank you (for coming),
thank you (for waiting), thank you (for being here),
thank you (for being his friend)

and I want to yell
I'm not his friend — I let him down.
He was *my* friend
and I let him drive away.

Unexpected

Just as the minister is about to start,
his book open in front of him,
a head bobs into view behind a break
in the crowd.
For a second I think it's Dean and relief floods through me.
But then another head, and another —
mourners turn and move aside —
and I recognize
a girl from my English class
and another guy who's a Legwarmer.

They stare at anything but the box
that holds James's body
and I can't take my eyes off them.

Then another clump of students dressed in black,
so their cliques are temporarily erased,
come into view from behind the hedge —
some girls already crying,
clutching their boyfriends
so they don't trip in their high heels.
Pretty soon
a group almost as big as the rest of us mourners
is crowded awkwardly
at one end of the congregation.
Guys stand uncomfortably in wrinkled suits

too big for their shoulders,
whisper to each other
as their girlfriends sob into wads of tissues
beside them.

I Feel Sick

but I'm standing in the front of the crowd,
next to the coffin and across from James's mother.
I can't make a scene.
The murmuring stops, the family sends grateful-sad smiles
across the space to the newcomers. *Oh good, James's friends
have come after all.*

No, I want to scream. Those tears aren't real.
Those guys never gave him a second glance —
those girls wouldn't be caught dead
speaking to him in the hall.
How dare they act sad — or even *be* sad —
they're hypocrites, pretenders.

They don't belong here.

Haiku: Car Ride Home

My fingernails dig
into soft leather as sun
dries my dripping face.

Phone Call from a Previous Life

Ashlyn's voice disconnects me

from my new normal.

But it's nice to hear her voice.

She asks suitably compassionate questions.

"I'm okay," I say automatically. *Okay as in empty.*

I rearrange the pillows on my bed

and sink into them.

When the socially appropriate amount of time

has elapsed, she starts blabbing about the Spring Fair,

short days away, and how hard everything
will be to pull off. Screw you, I think.
You don't know hard. Who the hell cares
about a stupid cake stall anyway?

But I listen to her soap opera stories
about batter and fondant. It takes me
out of my black thoughts.

"So, if you think about coming back to school,
it would be great to have your help."
I pick at a toothpaste blob on my shirt.
"If you feel up to it," she adds.
I roll onto my back and wish I could melt
inside the mattress.
"Or not — whatever you want."

I sigh.
Ashlyn pauses. "Look, I'm here, Gretchen. Call me
if you want to talk."

I wait until I know my voice won't waver,
say, "Thanks, Ashlyn,"
but I've already hung up the phone.

The Next Two Days

sleeping, staring, waiting, thinking, not thinking, not eating, crying, closing the curtains after Mum opened them, trying not to listen to Mum and Dad discuss me, my mental state, my academic state, my nutritional state. Layla's whines about going shopping and Mum's whispered response, *Stop it — can't you see it's not about you right now?* Wondering about Dean, worrying about Dean, battling myself not to call him ten times a day.

This Is Worse than the Grey Place

At least in the grey place
everything was frozen.
Nothing was harder than just *being*.
Now I'm stuck
in a new place
where everything *feels*.
And it's not just James.
Dean hasn't called
or emailed
or shown up
to say he's going to be okay now.

I go to bed exhausted
every night and wake up
still tired.

Blink

My parents
exchange sidelong glances
when they think
I'm not looking.
I'm always looking —
even when I sleep
I dream things I can't
turn away from.
James's face. His clean,
motionless hands.
Dean's curled-tight body
on the floor
of the hospital basement.

Sometimes I see
my own face
underwater, still and drowned.
I look so peaceful,
so unaffected.

Dear Gretchen,

I'm so sorry about your friend. I understand if you want to be alone right now, but
I wanted to say if you need a hug I'm here.
I'm not supposed to bug you and I don't want
to make you upset. I know I would be if I
lost one of my best friends. I'm just worried
about you. It's like you're someone else. If
you need to talk, or hug, I'm one door over.

Love, Layla

Eleven P.M.

On my way to the kitchen for a glass of water, I meet Layla
in the hall. She rubs her eyes en route to the bathroom.

"You . . . ?" she mumbles.

"Water," I say.

"Hmmm."

"Thanks," I say, "for the note."

"You're welcome."

She holds out her arms, like she assumes I want a hug
just because we're both in the same place so late at night.

But I walk into her scrawny kid frame and we hug and
hug and it feels good to be close to something so warm.

Family Dinner

The next night we sit down to our
macaroni and cheese with ham,
my dad's favourite, and we could be
any family. We pass the salt, we chat
about the weather, what to have for dessert.
Or: I listen while my family
does this. I focus on getting
food into my mouth. Even so, it tastes
like salty goo.

My sister keeps looking over at me
as if I'll blow up like a bomb.
I push away my plate.
Mum makes noises about my wasting away.
I make noises back, but she doesn't
agree with my reasoning.

Dad keeps his head down.
"Do you think you could go
to school on Monday?" he asks.
I feel the familiar stomach drop usually reserved
for chemistry tests.
I almost forgot school was my job in life.
It's clear they'll consider
forgoing the planned punishment
of hanging, drawing and quartering

in the hopes I will ease back
into school and be normal again.

I'll have to break it to them that I am not,
maybe never was, whatever normal means —
there was a geek inside me all the time.

The phone rings. It rings
like it's for me, so I get up.
Maybe it's Dean. I pray to hear
his voice on the other end.

"Gretchen? It's Ms Long. How are you?"
How random, I think.
But then I see it's not random.
My family stares at me hopefully.
I smell a setup.

Concern Morphs

through the phoneline from the tooth fairy's mouth into
my ear. She has the best "so sorry" voice.

"I know this might feel too soon, but it's important we
talk about what's going on, how you're feeling." She waits
for me to speak.

I don't.

"I'll try not to get all grown-up on you, Gretchen."

I walk into my room with the phone, and the comforting dark stuffiness envelops me. Why can't I just stay here forever?

"I know school might seem like a big thing right now, but how about we just meet for a chat?" She wants to meet in her office. I say no.

She suggests after school hours.

No.

She asks if I have any other words in my vocabulary.

"What do *you* want, Gretchen?" She waits.

I imagine her perched somewhere. I look at the clock; it's seven-fifteen. This can't be part of her job description. Tiny, committed Ms Long. An idea forms in the foggy recesses of my brain. I ask for her email address.

Her Name Is Jenny

I remember that from a letter I once saw
on her desk. I stare at my computer screen

for hours (it seems). How do I start this email?
Dear Jenny? Dear Jenny Long? Ms Long?

Dear Tooth Fairy sounds best, but then
I remember that Nemiah and I gave her that name
together —
god, I haven't seen Nemiah in so long.

Were we ever really friends? What does friends mean?

I pull the choking-throat feeling in
for later, when I can soak my pillow.

Dear Ms Long . . .

Walk in the Woods

When Layla and I were kids
we'd play in the ravine by our house
all day and all evening,

dragging ourselves home tired, hungry
and happy. We dreamed up new worlds
down there. And that's where I go

for my first real trip out of the house
in a week. The cedars rustle
in the wind and the air

smells like pine needles and wet dirt.
I wander the thin trail along the ravine,
which we used to think
was a huge valley. What other games
would we have played if James
and Dean had grown up with us?

I sit on a stump and the cold seeps
through my jeans. What would
we be doing right now

if he was still alive? I imagine
these non-moments, so perfect,
and the trees twist around me,

dropping needles.

Dear Gretchen,

I know nothing can really take away the
pain you're feeling, and I won't pretend I
can do that, but I thought these might be
something to read, to think about. They
helped me when I lost my father a few years
ago. The haiku masters really knew how
to make things resonate. I can lend you
a few more books of them if you like. And
keep writing. It seems to be helping you.

Ms Long

Insects on a bough
floating downriver,
   still singing.
         – Issa

That wren —
looking here, looking there.
   You lose something?
         – Issa

Coolness —
the sound of the bell
   as it leaves the bell.
         – Buson

Coming back —
so many pathways
   through the spring grass.
         – Buson

The Tooth Fairy's Other Office

My mother drops me at Ginger's coffee shop, hovers on the corner, unable to leave in case I get snatched up by bandits or just blow away in the wind. Ms Long sits in the window and waves as I walk up, and I wave at my mother, who inches away from the curb.

I order an apple cider and play with the stir sticks while it gets made. Now that I'm here I don't know what to say. What if she gets all Guidance Counsellor on me?

When I get to the table, she's poring over a gossip magazine. "You know, I hate this garbage," she says. "Here are the most expensive houses fought over in Hollywood — a six-page article." She looks up at me. "A waste of my time, right? And yet I read it." I slide into the empty seat. I tell her we're not allowed to read that stuff at my house. Ms Long pushes it over to me. "Then you need it more than I do."

We Talk

about the weather — how rainy/windy/cold it has been/ will be/should be. What we hate about school. Ms Long remembers high school really well for an adult — but then, she does work in one.

We dance around the subject of James for a long time by talking about poetry, and she hands me another book of haiku. I put it in my bag with the one I carry next to my wallet.

"James came to see me a few times," she says after a moment. "He had these fascinating theories about the social networks of high school."

I look out the window.

"But he had some rough days," she says. "When people don't understand something, exclusion or fear can drive their reactions."

"Is that what it was?" I mutter.

"What's that?" Ms Long peers at me.

"Nothing."

She waits. Glasses clink behind the coffee bar.

"They didn't know him," I say. "They judged and harassed him and made school hell for him."

"You were an antidote to that," she says.

"But I saw them do it. Three idiots on the lacrosse team. They cornered him every chance they got."

I put my mug down because my hands are shaking.

"They didn't kill him — you know that, right?"

"Well, he wouldn't be dead if they'd left him alone. And those kids at the funeral had the nerve to look sad — like they *knew* him. Those girls were sobbing like he was their brother!"

"Gretchen, you don't hold the patent on grief."

I want to smash something. "How can you defend them?"

Ms Long puts a hand on my knee. "I understand their reactions might seem false to you. I'm just saying that *everyone* is sad about James's death. The whole school is affected."

I take a breath. Two. "But why should the people who acted like he never existed, who laughed at him while he was standing in front of them, be able to grieve as if they're as broken as I am?"

Ms Long closes her eyes, as if to focus, before she speaks. "It was an accident, Gretchen. The road was incredibly slippery. The car that hit James was going way too fast. It's a tragedy and everyone knows that."

"No, they don't." I snap. "*They* know nothing about tragedy."

She Looks at Me

as if she's seeing something new,
something hard to look at.
I don't think what she's seeing
is something I want to be.

"You need to get past this," she whispers.
"Find a way — because I know you can —
to create a path out of this.

"I am here, your parents are here.
Any support you need you will have.
But you need to take the steps."
She takes my hands,
hers cool while mine are too warm.

"Poets are made for this.
You have it in you. Find it."

And in the End

when my mother arrives right on time
and Ms Long hugs me
before walking to her car,

I know she's right about one thing
at least.
Being this angry
isn't working for me.

I need to find
an exit.

14

WHO WE LOST

Two Days Later

I am sitting on the bus
in an area of town I don't know,
have never been to on my own
(small lie told about being with Ms Long),
going to a thing
I'm hoping can give me the key.
Rain lashes the bus windows
like a car wash.

Slamming

I sit close to the back, opposite side to last time,
behind a couple with dreadlocks and huge army boots.
It's louder, more crowded, more crazy this time.
I feel smaller, less sure I should have come.
But when the slam starts, I relax into the words,

into the banter and murmuring crowd,
the way the woman in front of me keeps squeezing her
friend's hand under the table.

The friend gets up to read, and her face — tired, wrinkled,
but beautiful —
reminds me of my mother's.
I feel impossibly homesick. I feel drowned.

She begins to read.

The Lost Boy

It's her son, dead of cancer at eleven,
who fills the spaces in and between her words
and jumps off the stage
as she brings him to life,
as she makes him
make us laugh and cry.
I see him standing there, listening.
He is James. He is this woman's son.
He is anyone who died too soon.

And it feels conceivable
that there is hope
at the bottom of all this.

I Have Become

a walker,
a step-at-a-time person.
An enjoyer of flowers,
clean air, good running shoes.

The other day I walked
for two hours, just through
the neighbourhood.
The places we used to think
were so boring and everyday.

Today I walk a new route,
along streets I've never seen,
and decide which house
I'd like to own. Cream with
dark blue trim. Front porch.
Bird bath in the front yard.

I stop at an intersection
and a mother with a stroller
pauses beside me. I glance
into the stroller, wondering
how cute the kid is,
and do a double take —
it's full of wriggling puppies.

Taken

The woman tells me the puppies' mother is missing. Someone stole her two days ago and the puppies are going to another dog who only has two babies so she can feed them.

The woman has pretty auburn hair and freckles and lets me pick up one of the pups. He squirms against me, warm and alive.

"We need to find their mom — they're not ready to leave her for another three weeks. And we miss her." The woman smiles sadly. She holds out a flyer, a lost poster, with the dog's name, Sasha, boldly on the top and a photo of her.

Under it are the usual details: age, last seen, friendly, affectionate.

Something clicks in my brain. I put the pup back with its siblings, thank her, and take a poster home.

I Am a Flurry of Art

I speak to no one,
hunch over my computer,
type, cut/paste, download
and with all the artistic talent I possess,

create.

LOST

JAMES TARDEN

LAST SEEN:
At Pins Bowling Alley, after being kicked out for a fight he didn't start

ALSO KNOWN AS:
Geek, Loner, Retarden

Funny and smart. Did college chemistry and math but was embarrassed to tell anyone. Thought the periodic table of elements was art. Hated cucumbers.

His family and friends miss him and want him back.

missing

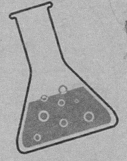

JAMES TARDEN

LAST SEEN:
On the Upper Levels Highway in his mother's Toyota Camry

ALSO KNOWN AS:
Loser, Freak, Weirdo

Loyal and kind. Planned to get a PhD in chemistry. A great tutor. Addicted to sour candies.

His family and friends miss him and want him back.

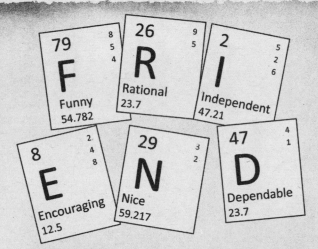

JAMES TARDEN

LAST SEEN:
Leaving school on a bus filled with kids who laughed behind his back

ALSO KNOWN AS:
Dork, Nerd, Craterface. James.

Helpful and lonely. Won a provincial science competition in grade 11. Carried old ladies' grocery bags across the street. Hated high school. Loved explaining the way things are.

His family and friends miss him and want him back.

15

WORD GETS AROUND

Monday: Return

I feel skittish and small
walking into school,
my backpack stuffed with lost posters
to be taped to walls.
My hope is they stay up for a few hours
until Mr. Cunningham, the principal,
sees them and takes them down. By then,
maybe someone will learn something
they didn't know before.

Strange Things

Ms Long meets me at my first class, English, to tell me that
if I feel sad or ill I can leave to find her. It's a little like kindergarten, but I feel safe. The bell hasn't rung yet and there
are five people in the class. None of them will look at me.
I grit my teeth and step into the hall. It's full. I stand there

for a minute feeling like wallpaper. Nothing has changed.

Then Garth/Thor from the cooking club walks up to me, makes some D&D hand signal I can't interpret and says somberly, "Gretchen, that poster is really cool. I literally almost cried. I'm sorry for being a loser that one day about you and —"

"It's okay," I say, trying not to sound like I ran up a flight of stairs. "Thanks."

And even though I don't hear a word of the English lesson, it feels not bad to be back.

Amazingly

most of the posters stay up for Tuesday, Wednesday, and by Thursday I'm getting looks in the hall, glances I can't quite place.

I hear James's name in the halls, and not as a point of ridicule. Mr. Marchand takes me aside to weep his gratitude that his star student has been immortalized with his favourite subject.

Mr. Cunningham calls me into his office and quietly congratulates me on a creative memorial. He commends me for using social media to get the word out. I stare at him blankly, think: *That would have been a good idea.* He shows me his computer screen, a page with photos of my posters, comments from people, dozens of likes.

Overkill?

Ashlyn meets me after French
and we walk to the cafeteria to get juice.
She fills me in on bakc sale news —
"and Gerry's got his aunt who owns
a bakery to donate some muffins, and
Julia will have a flat of doughnuts —
don't ask me where they're from —
and Mohammed's mother will make
these special cakes . . ."
She goes on and on, not even stopping
to drink her apple/cran. "So that's why
we're meeting at three —
to go over logistics."
I blink stupidly.
She grins at me. "That's a ton
of baked goods. We need more tables."
I sip my O. J. "But why are we getting donations?
I thought it was just us baking."
Ashlyn looks at me kindly,
like a grandmother
telling a toddler why rain falls.
"Gretchen, this is bigger than us.
It's bigger than The Foodies, even
this school." She grins. "Trust me.
We need more tables."

Something's Up

By P. E., almost the whole cooking club — and some people I don't even recognize — have come up to offer condolences and smile secret smiles about "three o'clock."

No one will tell me what this means. I feel blindfolded.

And it's not really a secret. Mr. Cunningham knows. The grad class knows (they smile at me too, but in a sad, I'm-glad-it's-you-and-not-me way).

Ms Long knows. She hugged me in the hall. People saw. I didn't care. I hugged her back.

We're Out in the Rain

playing something
that might resemble
field hockey. Mud
finds its way
into my socks, shorts,
ears and nose.
I manage to hit the ball
to someone who can score,
and then notice
Shay and Nemiah
talking behind the fence
at the edge of the field.

They look at me,

talk some more.
Shay shakes her head
and walks away. Nemiah
stands there for a second,
watching me
watch her.
She looks so small, so kidlike.

Someone yells behind me.
I run after the ball as it passes.
When I look back,
she's gone.

Cooking Club, 3:00 P.M.

Ms Long, little Ms Long
with horse teeth and perching, bird body
takes the floor. Her voice carries
around the room like she's got
a microphone.

The money from the bake sale
will go into a chemistry scholarship
in James's name.
She tells us how proud she is
of everyone, who has been working
on this for days.

Everyone looks so excited — more excited
than you'd think they would look
to be selling baked goods
for a dead boy's scholarship.

I glance at Ashlyn, who's beaming.
Suddenly I'm seeing her
from a different angle. Light is hitting her
in exactly the right places.

Insight

I'm treated to a welcome committee when I get home late
from organizing baked goods — Layla, Mum and Dad are
setting the table, tossing salad, pulling something spicy out
of the oven.

"Gretchen, we want to say —"

My mother is interrupted by Layla's bulldozing me
against the wall.

"You're so talented! I showed my class what you did."

"You showed what?" I ask.

"The posters! Mum and Dad got copies from Ms Long
and they printed some."

"You printed some?" I watch my parents' faces go from
proud to nervous to bashful.

Return

My phone is beside my head — I've been
expecting Ashlyn to call in a tizzy
about missing cream puffs —
and it rings me out of dreamless sleep.
His voice is low and scratchy.
I bolt awake. "Where are you?
Are you okay?"
There's music playing in the background.
"Look, I'm sorry for not calling," he says.
"I was an idiot when you were here."
He clears his throat. "I've really missed you."
We sit in silence, attached
by the phone, and even though I'm not the same
and he's not the same
and this conversation is awkward,
I miss him too.
"I need to see you," he says.
"Tomorrow's the Spring Fair."
"And you can't get away?"
I start to explain, but stop.
He clears his throat. "Can you meet me
in the morning? Just for a minute. I'll pick you up."
Something crunches on his end —
gravel underfoot.

16

APART TOGETHER

Dean Is Washed Out

like I've never seen him. Like a homeless ghost. His skin is grey and dry. His hair is greasy and flat against his head. He smiles at me from behind the wheel in a faintly Dean way. But I still wonder if it's actually him or if I'm being abducted by his alter ego — the guy who spat those terrible words at me in his apartment.

He reaches to hug me and at least he smells like him.

I ease back into the warm seat. The heater blows air into my face.

"You look good," he says as he pulls onto the street. "It feels like a year."

"Ten days can be a year," I say, stare out the window, watch the neighbourhood go by.

We Stop at Cleveland Dam Park

which isn't far from my house,
but far enough to make me feel
like I couldn't just run home.

We walk along the causeway
and look down at the loud water
spilling foam into the river below.

The mist that rises cuts through
my jacket. Dean puts his arm around me.
I wish we could just be this couple

looking at the water, wondering where
it came from. But we're both
in different worlds —

even though we touch, it's like
we're doing it from a distance.

Love?

We stand above the roar, letting the mist
drench our hair and the collars of our shirts
until we turn into trees. Our feet become roots
that burrow under the concrete and find soil
to eat and water to drink. We are entwined.
We are knotted trunks and reaching branches.

Dean pulls away first. He starts to tell me
how beautiful I am, but I'm hearing it
with different ears. Like the compliment
is something he's throwing at me.
I ask about the past few days, where he's been.
He closes his eyes. The tiny blue veins
on his lids pop out against his white-grey skin.

"I've been messed up. Just out of it."
I blink at him. "What does that mean?"
He shrugs, says, "I don't know."
But I know, then, as his hands shake a little
and his face twitches. He's high
or coming down, or something equally terrible.
There's nothing about him
I recognize.

But Still

I ask him to come
to the Spring Fair.
I reach for his cold hand
and tell him what the school,
the community, is doing
for James.

At the name
he freezes, locks his jaw.
I squeeze tighter,
but his hands are limp,
pulling away.
"I can't. I can't."
He swallows the rest
of the words.

 "Come on," I say.
"Your aunt will be there."

At this he snatches
his hands away.
I step forward. "But why not?"

Because

"I can't stand to see
them!" he shouts, red
in the whites of his eyes.
"Aunt Miriam
crying by the coffin —
his coffin —
a goddamn wooden box!
I can't do it."
He scrunches his face up,
pats his pockets
like he's looking
for something, then swears.
"I can't do it again."

"Wait — you were at the funeral?" I ask.
He looks so, so angry,
tear-someone's-head-off angry.
"Just for a minute, from outside.
It was so —"
He makes an animal sound,
a gut-wrenching,
dying sound
that goes over the edge,
roars with the foamy water
crashing into the canyon.

Haiku: For Dean

Boy-man, you try hard
to escape the sadness, but
it will bury you.

17

BAKED GOODS

Haiku: Chocolate Cake

Chunks eaten with milk,
no plate or fork, just family
mouths, hands reaching in

It Begins

School, Saturday morning: laden with boxes, already dusted in sugar, I'm amazed to see how many people are waiting.

It's not just a crowd. It's a small concert-worth. Students and parents and teachers and people who work at the grocery store and the hardware store and the gas station. They stand outside, line the halls and wander about, chatting.

"Gretchen!" Ashlyn literally runs into me. "Thank god you're here!"

"This is a madhouse!" I shout, putting my boxes down on the counter.

"We made some calls, but your posters have gone viral!" she screeches.

"I didn't put the page online with the posters," I yell over the din. "Did you?"

She shakes her head and shrugs. "Whoever did is a genius."

I've never seen her look so happy and so insane.

"How will we sell all this stuff?" I ask.

She just laughs. It's not about selling anymore. It's the principle.

Ms Long walks in grinning, weighed down with dough-nuts. We rush over before they topple.

The Fair

is on the playing field behind the school,
and with all the tables and booths and people,
you wouldn't think it was our field at all:
music playing from speakers somewhere,
the smell of popcorn, the slosh-splash of grads filling
a pool that will hold remote-controlled boat races.
The May air is warm, finally, and I can smell
flowers — probably because there's a stall selling
gardenware. I stand in the middle of all the chaos —
students, parents, teachers milling around me —
and just exist.

Everything Goes

not to plan, but that's okay because our plan
did not include fifty tonnes of baked good
donations this morning, or all the extra people
who've shown up to help.

Random people come up to me and say how
cool this is and that they like my posters.
Even Drama Queens with embryonic dogs in tow:
"We're totally going to buy a fruit tart later,
Gretchen," they giggle. "Are they low fat?"

I remind myself that this is more than
I could have hoped for — people who would have
ignored me before are saying they like
the posters, that they are sorry about James.

I can't magic high school into a place
where we all hold hands and get along.
James couldn't do it either,
even with his diagrams and theories.

But things aren't hopeless.

Suddenly

It's afternoon and I've been at the baking table for three hours.

Ms Long arrives, snags a brownie and squeezes my arm. "Nice shirt," she says. "Do I know who made it?"

I nod, looking down at the PoEM t-shirt James made me.

"This is actually perfect," Ms Long says. "I'm going to announce the scholarship in a few minutes. Mrs. Tarden is here —" she points and I see her walking toward us, her face tired but relaxed.

I cringe as Garth/Thor throws a date bar at some other kid's head. It hits the cash box and things dissolve from there.

"And I was hoping you could say a few words," Ms Long is saying. "In fact, it would be great if you could read a poem."

I choke on air. "What?"

"You've written some very eloquent poems about James. I just thought it might be fitting to read one here."

Now I know she's lost it. Great — the one person I thought I could count on.

"You wrote poetry about James?"

I swing around so fast I almost hit Mrs. Tarden, who's snuck up behind me and has a terribly hopeful look on her face.

She Asks Me to Read a Poem

and that is the worst thing, because I can't say no —
it's his mother, the woman
who smells like cinnamon and who knows
I understood her son,
and she knows I will say yes,
even if I say it by blushing and stammering.

This is the craziest thing
I have ever done — next to putting up lost posters
for a dead boy.
This isn't a poetry reading venue
or even a slam.
There can't be a crowd
more hostile to random acts of poetry.

Dizzy/Hyperventilating

I sit behind the baking table as Ms Long tells everyone that
there will be an announcement.

And an impromptu poetry reading — why doesn't she
say that? Maybe she's afraid that would send people running in the other direction. She'd be right. I lower my head
between my knees.

There's a tap on my shoulder. Garth/Thor breathes honey
doughnut breath into my ear. "Gretchen, on behalf of The
Foodies, and also my buddies in the D&D club, we want to

say we think you did a really kick-ass thing."

I turn and find about ten of the cooking club members, including a weeping Ashlyn, standing there.

"A lot of us acted like judgemental jerks. James was clearly a cool guy. We have to live with our, uh, jerkiness." Garth/Thor looks helplessly at the others. "But we're all really glad we can be here. We think this is a pretty cool way to have a memorial service."

Ms Long waves me to get up. She must have magical abilities because a crowd has gathered. A sizeable one.

Looking into Hell

I perch (Me! Perching!)
beside Ms Long,
who stands (Ms Long! Standing!)
in front of the baking tables.

Then she is speaking
about the scholarship
and blah blah blah
and soon it will be
my turn to form words,
and Mrs. Tarden is there,
smiling at us,
and my parents, Layla, waiting.
My eyes lock, without my permission,

onto the swim team congregation
(where did they come from?).
Shay stands in front, giggling.
She pokes a guy behind her,
who grabs her waist. Nemiah's dark head
peeks out between various broad torsos.

Something Slips

into my hand —
a piece of paper,
as Ms Long steps back,
urging me forward,
even though I'm too stunned
to look anywhere but at my shoes.
Until this moment
it hasn't occurred to me
that I didn't bring any poetry with me.
There's no time to think about
where the paper came from
because she's whispering,
"Forget they're here.
Read it to James."

18

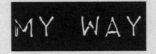

Where's Shakespeare?!

someone yells from the back of the crowd.
Others giggle. Feet shuffle.
Mumble mumble.
Oh my god.

Someone makes another joke
and Shay explodes in braying laughter —
now that I think about it,
she's always sounded like a donkey.

But the crowd
doesn't laugh with her.
Someone mutters *shut up, Shay* —
I'm shocked to see it's a lacrosse guy,
sneering at her in a way usually reserved
for the much less popular.

Someone else grabs her by the waist,
yanks her shrieking body
off the ground.
Throws her over his shoulder.

Her skinny butt wriggles
in the air, her boots kicking,
until she disappears
behind the crowd — who clap,
then cheer, then
stare at me.

Oh, right.
I'm on.

In My Hand

is a poem — my poem.
Until this second I had no idea
it would be the right thing
to read here, but it is.
No words I could have thought up
would be as good or as true.
Everything else would get stuck
in my mouth
like peanut butter.
These words are strong and black

on the page.
If I'm a poetry geek,
wearing it on my t-shirt for all to witness,
then so be it.

Intersections

Four corners, four directions,
where we stop and wait and go
and wait,
take turns deciding the way.
Last night you stood in the middle,
invisible to the cars
that drove through you,
around you.
I watched from one side
as you watched me.
You said nothing, your hands
open and still.

I thought:
this is the note, this is
the note. And when I woke up
I wondered, what was the note?

Your goodbye note to me.
The crossroads,
halfway to day, halfway to night,
the silent in-between.

You said: I'm going this way —
which way will you go?

There are different kinds of intersections.
Different notes for everyone.
All paths meeting, joining,
and parting again.

My way will be
because of you.
                    – Gretchen Meyers

Behind My Closed Eyelids

I see them gagging,

see them turning away,

I want to run,

find a hole to live in forever,

bad idea bad idea bad idea,

But . . .

Everyone Is Still Here

and the air has stopped buzzing.
No car engine, popcorn machine,
murmur or giggle.
Everything in the world
stops.
The crowd is silent
and I imagine us
breathing together, in and out.

And because it seems
like the only thing to do,
what Buson, Issa and Bashō
would do,
I imagine the words
floating up,
absorbed into the same cloud
that will rain on us later,
and the words will fall again
around us, like a new poem.

I didn't think it could happen,
but this is what he would have wanted.
What I want.
All of us, even though
it's not perfect,
the tormentors and bystanders

and victims,
the geeks — each of us one
in our own way,
being still,
being the same
because
we
are.

The Splash Heard Around the World

is the not-so-hot
leader of the swim team
being dumped
into the cold water
of the boat racing pool.

Rumour has it
you could see her patch
through her wet dress.

As We're Packing the Car

with doughnuts and muffins we don't need, I hear my
name across the parking lot. It's Nemiah. She runs up to
me in her funny way — until now I hadn't noticed her run
is so weird. I wonder if the swim team sees it.

She looks at my parents and Layla as if they might bite her. Mum gets into the car. They all do. We are alone beside the loaded trunk.

"I thought that was so amazing of you," she says. "I mean, so brave and everything. I've really missed that about you."

It's like she thinks I'll run away. But I've suddenly lost the will to hate her after all these months. We watch people leave the fair with their purchases and winnings. It's hard to know who should speak next.

"I'm sorry," she says, "about what happened with us. I was a loser."

"Yeah," I say. "You kind of were." It's impossible to find the right words, now the apology I've imagined since she left is actually happening.

She tries to smile. "Could we go for coffee?"

I don't have to speak to that. And I don't have to take her back. I nod. We'll see.

Inkling

As we leave, the school shrinking
behind us, houses flashing past,
exhaustion settling on me like a heavy blanket,
a hunch grows in my gut.

I am cliqueless, without a brand name,
but I have friends.

Better: I know what matters to me.
James showed me that.
I write what I know.
I have an inkling that might take me somewhere,
pen in hand.

I Call Dean

His voicemail picks up
and I take a deep breath.
"I just wanted you to know
how well it went at the fair.
Your aunt was so happy —
James has a scholarship
in his name. I feel like
he's happy too, wherever he is.
Enough sadness."

I pause, not sure what else to say.
The phone line crackles a little.
"Call me if you want to talk.
I'll always listen."

> *I go,*
> *you stay;*
> *two autumns.*
> - Buson

As I Drift Off

thinking of how much
I never want to see another
baked good again,

there's a little knock
on my door,
and Layla opens it
a crack and whispers,
"Cupcakes for breakfast tomorrow!"

Ashlyn's White Chocolate-Cherry Brownies

1 3/4 cups (430 mL) butter

1 1/2 cups (375 mL) dark chocolate chips or chunks

6 eggs

1 tablespoon (15 mL) vanilla

2 cups (500 mL) sugar

1 3/4 cups (430 mL) flour

1 teaspoon (5 mL) salt

2 cups (500 mL) white chocolate chips or chunks

1 cup (250 mL) dried cherries

Put the cherries into a saucepan, cover with water, and bring to a boil on the stove. Turn the heat off and leave the cherries to get plump in the water, about ten minutes.

Meanwhile, preheat the oven to 350 °F (160 °C). Line a baking pan (about 13 x 9 x 2 inches/33 x 23 x 5 cm) with baking parchment or foil.

Melt the butter and dark chocolate together in the microwave. In a large bowl, whisk the eggs with the sugar and vanilla. Measure the flour into another bowl and add the salt.

Add the slightly cooled chocolate mixture to the egg mixture and combine well. Then add the flour and mix to get a smooth batter. Add the white chocolate chunks.

Pour the batter into the prepared pan and smooth, making sure it's even all over.

Drain the cherries in a colander and press to get some of the water out of the fruit. Sprinkle the cherries over the brownie batter.

Bake in the oven for 30 to 35 minutes. Watch them closely and check to see if the centre is just solid, but not fully cooked; you want moist brownies, not dry ones. They will keep cooking as they cool.

Let the brownies cool completely before carefully using the sides of parchment as handles to lift onto a cutting board. Cut into squares. Find some friends to help you eat them.

Acknowledgements

Thank you
to those who helped this story grow
from a little idea to a bigger idea to a novel-sized idea:
Rachelle Delaney, Sheryda Warrener, Claire Tacon,
Alison Acheson, Keith Maillard, and to the Canada
Council for the Arts for their financial support

and those who generously shared their expertise
to make the story stronger:
my agent, Louise Lamont and editor, Anne Shone

and those who made sure the medical nitty was gritty:
Christina Mavinic, Kirsti Ziola

and those who have supported me from the very
beginning:
my mother, father and sister

and those who live with me every day
as I try to write the best things I can,
and whom I love with all my heart and both big toes:
my husband, Daryl, and daughter Elodie Pearl.

About the Author

Ria Voros is most definitely a poetry geek and a foodie. She is also a graduate of the University of British Columbia's Creative Writing MFA program and has published fiction and poetry internationally. Her first novel, *Nobody's Dog*, was published in 2012. Ria also teaches courses in fiction, poetry, literature and writing for children. When she isn't writing, Ria can be found cooking, hiking up mountains and gardening. She lives in Nanaimo, B. C., with her family.